P9-DHK-685

Letting Loose
the Hounds

Letting Loose
the Hounds

Stories

———————●———————

Brady Udall

W. W. Norton & Company
New York / London

For information about permission to reproduce selections from this book,
write to Permissions, W. W. Norton & Company, Inc., 500 Fifth Avenue,
New York, NY 10110.

The text of this book is composed in Granjon
with the display set in Tripley Condensed Serif.
Composition by Gina Webster on desktop using QuarkXpress 3.31
Manufacturing by Quebecor Printing, Fairfield Inc.
Book design by Chris Welch

Library of Congress Cataloging-in-Publication Data
Udall, Brady.
Letting loose the hounds : stories / Brady Udall.
    p.   cm.
ISBN 0-393-04033-X
I. Title.
PS3571.D36L48   1997
813'.54–dc20   96-18642
                    CIP

W. W. Norton & Company, Inc., 500 Fifth Avenue, New York, N.Y. 10110
http://www.wwnorton.com

W. W. Norton & Company Ltd., 10 Coptic Street, London WC1A 1PU

1   2   3   4   5   6   7   8   9   0

For Kate

Contents

Some of these stories originally appeared in the following publications, for which grateful acknowledgment is given:

Aethlon: "Junk Court"
Gentleman's Quarterly: "Midnight Raid"
The Midwesterner: "Vernon"
The Paris Review: "Letting Loose the Hounds"
Playboy: "Buckeye the Elder"
Story Magazine: "The Opposite of Loneliness," "Snake," "The Wig"
Sunstone: "Beautiful Places"

Thanks to the James Michener/Copernicus Society and the Henfield Foundation for their generous financial assistance, and to all the editors, teachers, friends, too numerous to name, who helped make these stories better. And deepest thanks to three people in particular: Nicole Aragi for doing the dirty work; Carol Houck Smith for humor and grace; Darrell Spencer for showing me how.

Letting Loose the Hounds

Midnight Raid

———————●———————

Roy growls and gives me the evil eye from inside his dog-house. He's flustered; I'm fairly certain this is the first time in his life a six-foot-three Apache Indian holding a goat has walked into his backyard in the middle of the night. Roy, there under the comfort of his own roof, seems to be trying to come to a decision. He doesn't know whether to raise hell or to make friends with me. I slowly take a step closer—no sudden moves—and ask him, as sincerely as possible, not to make any undue racket. He pokes his head out of his house and yaps, causing the goat I'm holding to let loose a thin stream of piss down my leg.

I suppose this ought to be explained: Roy is the pet of my ex-wife Amy and her new husband Howard, whose backyard I am currently lurking around in. The goat is a present for my seven-year-old son, Tate. Tate is somewhere in this immense, tacky house and my plan is to get this goat to him without Amy or Howard finding out about it. This is Scottsdale, Arizona, close to midnight and not too many degrees shy of a hundred. I would be untruthful if I didn't say I was a little drunk. I have dead grass in my hair and my belly feels like it's full of sharp sticks. Small, silvery fish are swimming around in my head, flashing behind my eyes like coins.

I'm positive that what I'm doing is the correct, the honorable thing. In that earnest, heartbreaking penmanship of his, my boy has written me at least half a dozen times asking for his pet goat, and no matter what my wife has to throw at me, the injunctions and restraining orders and so forth, I am going to get it to him.

"Roy," I say, looking up at this pink stuccoed mansion that's big enough for two zip codes, "where's Tate?"

Roy has no idea. And he's wondering how I know his name. Fact is, it's written in big capital letters above his little door, exactly the way they do it in cartoons. Roy tiptoes out of his house, his head cocked to one side, to have a better look at me. He's perplexed and not afraid to admit it. I hold out my hand, the universal peace offering, and he gives me a doubtful sniff. From the looks of him, Roy is not a pure breed of any kind. He has a thick, wedge-shaped head and bulging Marty Feldman eyes. His butt is as pink and hairless as a baboon's. He circles me once, paying particular attention to the goat. I think he's beginning to understand that neither of us are here to cause any harm.

Two lights are still on upstairs; I'm going to have to wait here until everything is dark and quiet before I make my move. Meantime, I'll sober up, gather my wits, get to know Roy a little. The backyard I'm in is nothing more than a football-field-sized patch of dry grass with a doghouse in the middle of it. There's no swing set or old soccer ball or anything else you'd expect to find in the yard in which a seven-year-old plays. Poor old Roy here doesn't even have a rubber bone to chew on. This is more a wasteland than a backyard, as if the soul of the desert still festers in this very spot, refusing to be driven out with sprinklers and lawnmowers and fertilizer. I sit down on the baked, crunching grass and look up at the drifting clouds that have been turned murky shades of orange and green by the lights of the city.

It would have been much more simple and comfortable to wait in front of the house in my air-conditioned truck, but this beefy woman security guard kept walking by, asking what my business in the neighborhood was. I made up elaborate lies about a surprise party for my mother-in-law who lived just down the street. Pretty soon she started asking for names and addresses. She wanted to see some identification. I mumbled and coughed and acted drunker than I was and she told me I'd have to leave or she'd call the cops. So I parked my truck at a mini-mall about a mile away and came in on foot, sticking to the shadows and bushes, the goat hee-hawing and complaining the whole time. I had to be particularly careful because nearly all the houses around here have huge floodlights, as powerful as the kind you might find at Yankee Stadium, that are specifically designed to keep people like me away.

Theoretically, the art of sneaking and hiding and stealing through the night should be in my blood. I'm three-quarters Apache, a registered member of the White Mountain tribe. They say my ancestors could melt into the underbrush, run at full speed without making a sound, crouch as still as a tree stump for hours on end. Soldiers of the U.S. Army used to swear that the Apache had the power to make themselves invisible. Right now, I would settle for just being able to keep this goat quiet.

I never lived the Apache lifestyle, even by today's standard; I grew up in a middle-class section of Winslow where my father worked at the post office. Most of my extended family lives on the reservation and when I go to visit they all laugh at me. They tell me I talk like John Wayne. The say I smell like a department store. And I married a white woman which did not go over too well. What has being an Indian meant to me? A scholarship from UCLA, a boring job at an electronics firm and suspicious looks from the clerk whenever I go into a 7-11.

Most everybody thinks that the breakup happened because of the pressures and conflicts that go along with an interracial marriage. Actually, this had nothing to do with it at all. Our divorce was an honest, smash-mouth affair based on past indiscretions and betrayals on both our parts. Until the very end we went on pretending that everything was perfect, never looking one another in the eye. Then one day my wife came home and accused me of "malfeasance." Right then I knew it was all over. You don't come into your own home throwing around words like "malfeasance" unless you've been talking to lawyers. Amy got the boy, our classic Cadillac and most of the money, leaving me with the house and the pickup. Now she's married to a retired rancher who has the money to waste on lawyers who have the arcane ability to twist the law, make it so that a father cannot even see his own son. "Damn the law," I say to Roy. "Damn the Constitution." Roy licks his chops and doesn't disagree.

In the backyard that adjoins this one somebody has begun making a racket, splashing around in their pool and burping and singing snatches of old Sinatra songs in a way that is painful to hear. After awhile I can't stand it anymore and I walk over to the fence—it's quite a long walk—with Roy following behind. The fence is much too high to see over so I just have to yell, "Will you put a lid on it over there?"

"Who said that?" the guy calls out. By his voice I'd guess he's around retirement age and has a good bit of beer in him.

"Over here," I say.

"Are you my neighbor?"

"I could be."

"What's the yelling for?"

"It's to quiet you down."

"I think you're just jealous of this nice pool I've got. You're the only goddamn one in this whole goddamn neighborhood without a pool. It's common knowledge around here."

I don't have anything to say to that so I keep my mouth shut.

"Well, why?" he says.

"Why what?"

"Why don't you have a pool?"

I think about it for a minute. "Because I'm a horse's ass."

"Ten-four," he says.

I go back to my spot next to Roy's doghouse and sit down on this lawn that's as soft and inviting as the bottom of a skillet. It really makes me wonder what kind of sense Amy and this Howard character have. What's the point in living in a place like this, knocking elbows with the rich and the famous, and not owning a pool? I could be taking a few laps and cooling off while I wait instead of sitting here, covered with a grainy film of sweat and smelling like a world war. I think if I was the goat I'd be complaining too.

Tate loves this damn goat more than anything in the world and for reasons I can't understand, Amy won't let him have it. I've fought with her about it, called her up on the phone and told her that for a child to grow up without a pet is not right. She told me Tate had a pet, a dog that he got along with rather

well. Tate wrote me a letter to set the record straight. He said
he didn't like the dog much at all; it was ugly and stupid and
had bugs living in its fur. Though Roy does have his positive
qualities, I would have to say Tate had him pegged pretty
good. *All I want*, Tate wrote, *is Jumpy, my goat.* That tore my
heart in two meaty halves, brought water to my eyes, and here
I am, doing what I can to make my boy happy.

As long as the truth is coming out all over the place, I might
as well admit that the goat I'm holding in my arms, the one
Roy is sniffing warily right now, is not the original Jumpy.
Tate found the original Jumpy tangled in some barbed wire
near our home in Flagstaff. We were never able to find the
owner so Tate kept it. It was a cute little thing, so tiny, with its
flopping ears and old man's beard. Tate loved it so much he
kept it in his room for the first few days, put Pampers on it
and fed it with a bottle. After the stink got to be too bad I built
a small pen for it out back. A few months passed and we
noticed that it wasn't growing at all. We took it to the vet and
he told us it was not a baby goat as we'd thought all along, but
an adult pygmy goat. He held up one of its hind legs and said,
"See there? Fully developed gonads."

"Adult?" we said. "Gonads?"

The vet said, "Adult as it gets. It's a pygmy goat. It's small.
That's the point."

We didn't have the heart or the know-how to explain to
Tate that this cute little pet of his was not an innocent baby,
but an adult with an active sex drive, fully developed gonads
and the whole bit. We let him live with that childhood notion
that it's possible for things to stay the same, that everything in
this world does not have to become old and tired and undone.

When Amy left with Tate, she wouldn't let him take
Jumpy. Maybe, like me, she saw the goat as a symbol or a
reminder of something: our shared life, our togetherness.

They went away and I never fed the goat again. I don't know how long it was before it died; I stopped going to work, I was drunk and fairly deranged twenty-four hours a day. I came unglued; there were pieces of me all over my suddenly too-large house. I wandered room to room, shuffling my feet and knocking things over like a clumsy ghost. One day I looked out the window. Down in Jumpy's pen were several buzzards and some crows all crammed in a huddle as if discussing secret matters. I grabbed my shotgun, intent on blowing those carrion-eaters into next Sunday, but in my condition I couldn't even find the safety on the gun and those evil birds got away scot-free. Jumpy was just a little pile of bones that looked like the remains of somebody's chicken dinner. He had eaten every last weed and blade of grass inside his pen and the bark on the lower sections of the cedar fence posts had been completely chewed away. Right then I would have turned the gun on myself had I been able to locate the goddamn safety.

I let almost a year go by before the guilt, eating at my insides like an ulcer, drove me to do something about it. It took two weeks, around four dozen phone calls and a three-hundred-mile trip to Albuquerque to find a pygmy goat that looked anything similar to Jumpy. The guy that sold it to me was an old Mexican bean farmer with unnecessarily perfect teeth. I guess he could see the desperation running rampant on my face and he couldn't stop smiling about it. He told me he wouldn't part with this goat for less than one hundred and thirty-three dollars. He said he had special feelings for this particular animal and to give it up to a stranger like me would cause considerable pain no matter what the price. I coughed up ninety dollars—it was all I had to spare—and on my way down here I stopped at a Burger King and bought the goat a Whopper, some fries and a shake.

We've been together two days now and this goat is beginning to get to me. Sometimes, for no reason at all, it raises its
tiny head and lets out a high-pitched squall that sounds like
the screech of car tires. It has already bitten all the buttons off
my shirt and swallowed them, not to mention the pissing and
shitting every half hour. Roy, who apparently has come to the
conclusion that neither of us provide any great threat, sits
right next to me, his butt jammed against mine, and looks up
at me with these glossy, rolling eyes. I give him a squeeze. We
all need love and Roy is no different. He sighs in my face and
I inform him his breath could be better.

Both of the lights upstairs go off within seconds of each
other. I get up and wander around the back of the house,
checking the windows and the sliding glass door. All locked.
A dry, cottony panic expands in my throat, shutting off my
air. I had this crazy idea in my head that I could just crawl
through a window, locate Tate in the slumbering household,
leave the goat with him and be on my way. This was the plan
I came up with after a few rounds of tequila at the bar earlier
this evening. Now that I'm bordering on sober, I'm aware that
~~that~~ it's not going to work. No doubt Howard has an alarm
system rigged up to protect his house; Amy wouldn't just
marry any idiot. And if there's one thing I don't want, it's to
get the police involved.

I lie down on the grass and squeeze my head between my
hands, trying to think. Lord, this heat! Hell could not do much
better than this. It feels as if all the moisture has been sucked
out of my brain, leaving it as useless as a punctured football. My
teeth and eyeballs are like old wood. Roy comes over and goes
to work licking my face. I take an after-dinner mint from my
jeans pocket and give it to him. He gnashes it into a fine green
paste, smiles at me and waits for another. I pull my pockets
inside out to illustrate there is no more where that came from.

My watch tells me it's already one a.m. I have to do something—I can't spend all night commiserating with a dog in
this pounding heat. I stand up and look around for something
to throw; there's nothing in the grass, not so much as a stick or
a pebble. I peel one of the tar shingles off Roy's doghouse and
sling it like a Frisbee at what I hope will be Tate's window.
The shingle misses by a good five feet and *thwaps* against the
side of the house, causing a shower of stucco dust to float to
the grass like pink snow. For some reason this sends Roy into
a barking frenzy and before I can get him quieted down a
light comes on upstairs. I crouch behind the doghouse, my
chin between my knees. I hear a window slide open and Amy
say, "Roy, will you shut up?" in that beautiful voice of hers
that sounds like rain falling on a lake. Back when we were
going out I used to call her answering machine when she was-
n't home just to listen to the puff and slide of her vowels.

I can't help myself. Staying where I am I say, "Rapunzel,
Rapunzel, let down your hair."

There is a long, thunderous silence before she says, "Jerry?"

I stand up. No more sneaking around like a coward. I pick up
the goat and say, "I'm here to—I brought this—I'm absolutely
serious, dammit."

She is a black cut-out against the light behind her. I can tell
she is straining to see; she takes her contacts out before she
goes to bed. She whispers, "Oh, Lord."

She moves away from the window and seconds later a light
blinks on in the living room. I tuck my shirt in and try to
shake the debris out of my hair. She opens the door and sticks
her head out. She's wearing black-rimmed glasses and an
expression of bewilderment. Roy barks happily and the goat
gives me a solid kick in the ribs, a blow akin to being jabbed
in the midsection with the fat end of a pool cue. Howard
appears at the top of the stairs and begins an uneven, thump-

ing descent. From this distance, he looks younger than his sixty-one years. His skin is the polished bronze Hollywood actors would sell their souls for.

Holding my gut, I push the door open and step inside. A frosty air-conditioned current swirls over me and it's as if I've just stumbled into heaven. I shut the door behind me so as to not let any of this wonderful air out. Roy puts his nose on the glass and looks up at me as if I've betrayed him.

"For God's sake, Jerry," Amy says. Why would she have to be wearing the green satin nightgown I bought for her birthday a few years ago? This is the nightgown that shows up in a good many of my fondest memories. I can smell the aloe lotion she likes to use on her skin.

"I brought this goat, for Tate," I say. My voice is a wounded, struggling thing in the cool elegance of this living room. "Just two minutes to give him the goat and say hello and I'm gone. You won't even notice me."

Howard limps up next to Amy and I see under the hem of his bathrobe that he has one normal, tanned leg and one that is made of shiny, flesh-colored plastic. His white hair is like the bristles on a toilet brush. Can it be that my wife left me to marry this liver-spotted senior citizen with dentures and an artificial leg? Then I remember how rich the son of a bitch is and it makes me feel a little better.

"Would someone kindly inform me as to what in the name of hell is going on here?" he says. If it is possible to make a western drawl sound refined and high-minded, then this guy is pulling it off. We are standing on a circular rug that is made from the hides of at least six cows. Expensive Navajo rugs hang from almost every wall.

"Is Tate's room upstairs?" I ask.

"Now wait right there, son," Howard says, standing between me and the foot of the staircase. "You're breaking the law here. You've just entered my house without permission and broken the terms of the restraining order placed on you last month. You're up shit creek and sinking fast."

Did he call me "son"? I look at Amy to see if she is as astounded by this as I am. Her arms are folded over her chest and she's chewing on her thumbnail—*tick tick tick*—a habit that used to drive me crazy until I bought her a self-help book that aided her in finding the inner power to stop.

I start for the stairs and Howard blocks my way, resting his hand lightly on my shoulder. He gives me this terrifically sincere look and says, "You and the farm animal are invited to leave."

I shift the goat to my left arm and hit him in the mouth with my right. He teeters for a moment on his good leg, his lower lip already sprouting blood, before he goes down. I know that he is handicapped and older than my own father, but who ever accused an Apache of fighting fair? Maybe when everything is finished Howard will count himself lucky that he made it through this whole situation without getting scalped.

What I feel climbing the stairs is not the mindless, teeth-grinding anger that usually rises up when I'm in a situation that involves confrontation and punches and blood. At first the only thing inside me is the blinders-on determination that I'm not leaving this house without seeing my son, but something else comes over me, a sudden ache of sadness at the measures we have to take, the desperations and last resorts. I feel an unwieldy heaviness, all thirty-eight years of me pressing down, and as I haul myself up those last few steps it's all I can do to keep from dropping the goat down the stairs.

I open all the doors in the upstairs hallway and the last one is Tate's; I can tell it instantly by the smell of dirty socks and model airplane glue. I put the goat down and kneel by his bed in the strip of light coming in from the hall. Can there be anything more sweet and beautiful than a sleeping child, especially your own? He snorts and rubs his face in his Robocop pillow, oblivious to the adult idiocy going on around him. Amy stands in the doorway for a second, most likely to make sure that I'm not doing anything drastic, and I have this terrible sense of *déja vu:* after dinner and TV, Tate wrapped up in his covers, me telling boring stories about my college years in the hopes it will put him to sleep, Amy looking in on the both of us.

When I glance up again Amy is gone. I can hear her downstairs exchanging whispers with Howard. Looking down at my sleeping son, feeling his heart vibrating through the blanket, I'm nearly paralyzed with the thought that in a matter of minutes I'll be forced to walk away, leave him here in this strange room, in this strange house. It takes what little strength I have left to move away from the bed, turn on a lamp, retrieve the goat from over by the desk where it's chewing on one of Tate's baseball cards. I empty out his toy box and put the goat inside so it won't be able to run loose. I sit down at his miniature desk and write him a short note with the only writing instrument available, a fat neon-green marker shaped like a dancing dragon. In a shaky, trailing hand I remind him to make sure to feed the goat every day and to mind his mother. I tell him that I love him and to remember me in his prayers. Before leaving, I tidy up his room a little.

Downstairs, Howard is on the phone, blood smeared on his chin and a shiny old-style silver and gold pistol dangling from one hand, explaining calmly and eloquently to the police that an intruder, a crazed Indian no less, has violated the sacred boundaries of his home. He informs them that if someone does not arrive on the double, he may be obliged to use the kind of deadly force you read about in the newspapers.

I stand at the bottom of the stairs unsure of what to do next. Amy is nowhere to be seen. I know I should get out of here fast if I don't want to be making conversation with druggies and car thieves in the county jail tonight, but first I feel something has to be said, some apology made.

Howard puts down the phone and says, making sure I can see the gun in his hand, "Are you on your way out?"

Unable to come up with anything better, I say, "This is a real nice house you've got here, Howard."

Amy appears out of the kitchen with a glass of scotch in her hand. She stares at me blankly, as if I'm a salesman who has entered her house to demonstrate a product she has no interest in.

"You might think about getting a pool, though," I say. "A pool would be nice."

"I can't swim," Howard says.

"It's late," Amy sighs, pinching the bridge of her nose with her thumb and forefinger.

"Migraine?" I say.

She says, "Please, Jerry."

"Okay, yep, no problem." I'm talking on my way to the front door just to fill the silence. "I better be leaving. Bye-bye."

Once Howard has shut the door on me and I'm outside, empty-handed and loping across the scorching street, I feel more lonely and lost than I ever have in my life; it's as if I've been completely scraped out from the inside. I make it to the end of the block before I do a one-eighty and sprint back to Amy and Howard's backyard. I open the gate and Roy is waiting right there as if he knew I would return. "You want to come?" I whisper and he goes haywire, huffing and yapping, his tail whipping all over the place. He ricochets off my chest and runs around in a tight circle. I take out my pocket-knife and scratch a few words above the name on his doghouse so it reads like a short farewell letter:

I'm long gone
Love,
ROY

I grab hold of his collar and lead him out into the street. I don't have a leash, but he stays right with me, his shoulder sporadically bumping my leg. We're trotting across someone's front lawn when I have to pull him into the bushes to let a patrol car go by, lights pulsing. I get my wind back and we're off again, ducking and sprinting from house to house, dodging through sprinklers and hiding behind an occasional decorative cactus, keeping to the shrubbery and shadows when we can.

Buckeye the Elder

———————————o———————————

Things I learned about Buckeye a few minutes before he broke my collarbone: he is twenty-five years old, in love with my older sister, a native of Wisconsin and therefore a Badger. "Not really a Buckeye at all," he explained, sitting in my father's recliner and paging through a book about UFOs and other unsolved mysteries. "But I keep the name for respect of the man who gave it to me, my father and the most loyal alumnus Ohio State ever produced."

Buckeye had stopped by earlier this afternoon to visit my sister, Simone, whom he had been seeing over the past week or so. Though Simone had yammered all about him over the dinner table, it was the first time I'd actually met him. When he arrived, Simone wasn't back from her class at the beauty college and I was the only one in the house. Buckeye came inside for a few minutes and talked to me like I was someone he'd known since childhood. He showed me old black-and-white photos of his parents, a gold tooth he found on the floor of a bar in Detroit, a ticket stub autographed by Marty Robbins. Among other things, we talked about his passion for rugby and he invited me out to the front yard for a few lessons on rules and technique. Everything went fine until tackling came up. He positioned himself in front of me and instructed me to try to get around him and he would demonstrate the proper way to wrap up the ball player and drag him down. I did what I was told and ended up with two hundred-plus pounds worth of Buckeye driving my shoulder into the hard dirt. We both heard the snap, clear as you please.

"Was that you?" Buckeye said, already picking me up and setting me on my feet. My left shoulder sagged and I couldn't move my arm but there wasn't an alarming amount of pain. Buckeye helped me to the porch and brought out the phone so I could call my mother, who is on her way over right now to pick me up and take me to the hospital.

I'm sitting in one of the porch rocking chairs and Buckeye is standing next to me, nervously shifting his feet. He is the picture of guilt and worry; he puts his face in his hands, paces up and down the steps, comes back over to inspect my shoulder for the dozenth time. There is a considerable lump where the fractured bone is pushing up against the skin.

A grim-faced Buckeye says, "Snapped in two, not a doubt in this world."

He puts his face right into mine as if he's trying to see something behind my eyes. "You aren't in shock are you?" he says. "You don't want an ambulance?"

"I'm okay," I say. Other than being a little light-headed, I feel pretty good. There is something gratifying about having a serious injury and no serious pain to go with it. More than anything, I'm worried about Buckeye, who is acting like he's just committed murder. He's asked me twice now if I wouldn't just let him swing me over his shoulders and run me over to the hospital himself.

"Where is my self-control?" he questions the rain gutter. "Why can't I get a hold of my situations?" He turns to me and says, "There's no excuses, none, but I'm used to tackling guys three times your size, God forgive me. I didn't think you'd go down that easy."

Buckeye has a point. I am almost as tall as he is but am at least sixty pounds lighter. All I really feel right now is embarrassment for going down so easy. I tell him that it was nobody's fault, that my parents are generally reasonable people, and that my sister will probably like him all that much more.

Buckeye doesn't look at all comforted. He keeps up his pacing. He thinks aloud with his chin in his chest, mumbling into the collar of his shirt as if there is someone down there listening. He rubs his head with his big knobby hands and gives himself a good tongue-lashing. There is an ungainly energy to the way he moves. He is thick in some places, thin in others and has joints like those on a backhoe. He's barrel-chested, has elongated piano player's fingers and is missing a good portion of his left ear which was ground off by the cleat of a stampeding Polynesian at the Midwest Rugby Invitationals. I can't explain this, but I'm feeling quite pleased that Buckeye has broken my shoulder.

When my mother pulls up in her new Lincoln, Buckeye picks up me and the chair I'm in. With long, smooth strides he delivers me to the car, all the time saying some sort of prayer, asking the Lord to bless me, heal me, and help me forgive.

One of the more important things that Buckeye didn't tell me about himself that first day was that he is a newly baptized Mormon. I've found out this is the only reason my parents ever let him within rock-throwing distance of my sister. As far as my parents are concerned, solid Baptists that they are, either you're with Jesus or you're against him. I guess they figured that Buckeye, as close as he might be to the dividing line, is on the right side.

In the week that has passed since the accident, Buckeye has turned our house into a carnival. The night we came home from the hospital, me straight-backed and awkward in my brace and Buckeye still asking forgiveness every once in awhile, we had a celebration—in honor of who or what I still can't be sure. We ordered pizza and my folks, who almost never drink, made banana daiquiris while Simone held hands with Buckeye and sipped ginger ale. Later, my daiquiri-inspired father, once a 163-pound district champion in high school, coaxed Buckeye into a wrestling match in the front room. While my sister squealed and my mother screeched about hospital bills and further injury, Buckeye wore a big easy grin and let my father pin him solidly on our mint-green carpet.

I suppose there were two things going on: we were officially sanctioning Buckeye's relationship with Simone and at the same time commemorating my fractured clavicle, the first manly injury I've ever suffered. Despite and possibly because of the aspirations of my sports-mad father, I am the type of son who gets straight A's and likes to sit in his room and make models of spaceships. My father dreamed I would play for the Celtics one day. Right now, having just finished my sophomore year in high school, my only aspiration is to write a best-selling fantasy novel.

My sister goes to beauty school, which is a huge disappointment to my pediatrician mother. Simone can't bear to tell people that my father distills sewer water for a living. Even though I love them, I sincerely believe my parents to be narrow-minded religious fanatics and as for Simone, I think beauty school might be an intellectual stretch. As far as I can tell, our family is nothing more than a bunch of people living in the same house who are disappointed in each other.

But we all love Buckeye. He's the only thing we agree on. The fact that Simone and my parents would go for someone like him is surprising when you consider the coarse look he has about him, the kind of look you see on people in bus stations and in the backs of fruit trucks. Maybe it's his fine set of teeth that salvages him from looking like an out-and-out redneck.

Tonight Buckeye is taking me on a drive. Since we first met, Buckeye has spent more time with me than he has with Simone. My parents think this is a good idea; I don't have many friends and they think he will have a positive effect on their agnostic, asocial son. We are in his rust-cratered vehicle that might have been an Oldsmobile at one time. Buckeye has just finished a day's work as a pantyhose salesman and smells like the perfume of the women he talks to on porches and doorsteps. He sells revolutionary no-run stockings that carry a lifetime guarantee. He's got stacks of them in the back seat. At eighteen dollars a pair, he assures these women, they are certainly a bargain. He is happy and loose and driving all over the road. He has just brought me up to date on his teenage years, his father's death, the thirteen states he's lived in and the twenty-two jobs he's held since then.

"Got it all up here," he says, tapping his forehead. "Don't let a day slide by without detailed documentation." Over the past few days I've noticed Buckeye has a way of speaking that makes people pause. One minute he sounds like a West Texas oil grunt, the next like a semi-educated Midwesterner. Buckeye is a constant surprise.

"Why move around so much?" I wonder. "And why come to Texas?"

He says, "I just move, no reason that I can think of. For one thing, I'm here looking for my older brother Bud. He loves the Cowboys and fine women. He could very well be in the vicinity."

"How'd your father die?" I say.

"His heart attacked him. Then his liver committed suicide and the rest of his organs just gave up after that. Too much drinking. That's when I left Wisconsin for good."

We are passing smelters and gas stations and trailers that sit back off the road. This is a part of Tyler I've never seen before. He pulls the old car into the parking lot of a huge wooden structure with a sign that says "The Ranch" in big matchstick letters. The sun is just going down but the place is lit up like Las Vegas. There is a fleet of dirty pickups overrunning the parking lot.

We find a space in the back and Buckeye leads me through a loading dock and into the kitchen where a trio of Hispanic ladies is doing dishes. He stops and chatters at them in a mixture of bad Spanish and hand gestures. "Come on," he says to me. "I'm going to show you the man I once was."

We go out into the main part which is as big as a ballroom. There are two round bars out in the middle of it and a few raised platforms where some half-dressed women are dancing. Chairs and tables are scattered all along the edges. The music is so loud I can feel it bouncing off my chest. Buckeye nods and wags his finger and smiles at everybody we pass and they respond like old friends. Buckeye, who's been in Tyler less than a month, does this everywhere we go and if you didn't know any better you'd think he was acquainted with every citizen in town.

We find an empty table against the wall right next to one of the dancers. She has on lacy black panties and a cutoff

T-shirt that is barely sufficient to hold in all of her equipment. Buckeye politely says hello, but she doesn't even look our way.

This is the first bar I've ever been in and I like the feel of it. Buckeye orders Cokes and buffalo wings for us both and surveys the place, once in awhile raising a hand to acknowledge someone he sees. Even though I've lived in Texas since I was born, I've never seen so many oversized belt buckles in one place.

"This is the first time I've been back here since my baptism," he says. "I used to spend most of my nonworking hours in this barn."

While he has told me about a lot of things, he's never said anything about his conversion. The only reason I even know about it is that I overheard my parents discussing Buckeye's worthiness to date my sister.

"Why did you get baptized?" I say.

Buckeye squints through the smoke and his voice takes on an unusual amount of gravity. "This used to be me, sitting right here and drinking till my teeth fell out. I was one of these people—not good, not bad, sincerely trying to make things as easy as possible. A place like this draws you in, pulls at you."

I watch the girl in the panties gyrating above us and I think I can see what he's getting at.

He continues: "But this ain't all there is. Simply is not. There's more to it than this. You've got to figure out what's right and what's wrong and then you've got to make a stand. Most people don't want to put out the effort. I'm telling you, I know it's not easy. Goodness has a call that's hard to hear."

I nod, not to indicate that I understand what he's saying, but as a signal for him to keep going. Even though I've had my fair share of experience with them, I've never understood religious people.

"Do you know what life's about? The *why* of the whole thing?" Buckeye says.

"No more than anybody else," I say.

"Do you think you'll ever know?"

"Maybe someday."

Buckeye holds up a half-eaten chicken wing for emphasis. "Exactly," he says through a full mouth. "I could scratch my balls forever if I had the time." He finishes off the rest of his chicken and shrugs. "To know, you have to do. You have to get out there and take action, put your beliefs to the test. Sitting around on your duff will get you nothing better than a case of the hemorrhoids."

"If you're such a believer, why don't you go around like my parents do, spouting scripture and all that?" I reason that if I just keep asking questions I will eventually get Buckeye figured out.

"For one thing," Buckeye says flatly, "and you don't need to go telling this to anybody else, but I'm not much of a reader."

I raise my eyebrows.

"Look here," he says, taking the menu from between the ketchup and sugar bottles. He points at something on it and says, "This is 'a', this is a 't' and here's a 'g.' This says 'hamburger'—I know that one. Oh, and this is 'beer.' I learned that early on." He looks up at me. "Nope, I can't read, not really. I never stayed put long enough to get an education. But I'm smart enough to fool anybody."

If this were a movie and not real life I would feel terrible for Buckeye—maybe I would vow to teach him to read, give him self-worth, help him become a complete human being. For the climax he would win the national spelling bee or something. But this is reality and as I look across the table at Buckeye, I can see that his illiteracy doesn't bother him a bit. In fact, he looks rather pleased with himself.

"Like I've been telling you, it's not the reading, it's not the saying. It's only the doing I'm interested in. Do it, do it, do it," Buckeye says, hammering each "do it" into the table with his Coke bottle. He leans into his chair, a wide grin overtaking his face. "But sometimes it certainly is nice to kick back and listen to the music."

We sit there quiet for awhile, me doing my best not to stare at the dancer and Buckeye with his head back and eyes closed, sniffing the air with the deep concentration of a wine judge. A pretty woman in jeans and a flannel shirt comes up behind Buckeye and asks him to dance. There are only a few couples out on the floor. Most everybody else is sitting at their tables, drinking and yelling at each other over the music.

"Thanks but no thanks," Buckeye says.

The woman looks over at me. "What about you?" she says.

I panic. My face gets hot and I begin to fidget. "No, no," I say. "No, thank you."

The woman seems amused by us and our Cokes. She takes a long look at both of us with her hands on the back of an empty chair.

"Go ahead," Buckeye says. "I'll hold down the fort."

I shake my head and look down into my lap. "That's quite all right," I say. I don't know how to dance and the brace I'm wearing makes me walk like I've got arthritis.

Buckeye sighs, smiles, gets up and leads the woman out onto the floor. She puts her head on his chest and I watch them drift away, swaying to the beat of a song about good love gone bad.

When the song is over Buckeye comes back with a flushed face and a look of exasperation. He says, "You see what I mean? That girl wanted things and for me to do them to her. She wanted these things done as soon as possible. She asked me if I didn't want to load her bases." He plops down in his chair and drains his Coke with one huge swallow. It doesn't even make him blink.

On our way home he pulls into the deserted front lot of a drive-in movie theater and floors the accelerator, yanking the steering wheel all the way over to the left and holding it there. He yells, "Carnival ride!" and the car goes round and round, pinning me to the passenger door, spitting up geysers of dust and creaking and groaning as if it might fly into pieces at any second. When he finally throws on the brakes, we sit there, the great cloud of dust we made settling down on the car, making ticking noises on the roof. The world continues to hurtle around me and I can feel my stomach throbbing like a heart.

Buckeye looks over at me, his head swaying back and forth a little and says, "Now doesn't that make you feel like you've had too much to drink?"

Simone and I are on the roof. It's somewhere around midnight and there are bats zooming around our heads. We can hear the *swish* as they pass. I have only a pair of shorts on and Simone is wearing an oversized T-shirt. The warm grainy tar paper holds us against the steep incline of the roof like Velcro. Old pipes have forced us out here. Right now these pipes, the ones that run through the north walls of our turn-of-the-century house, are engaged in their semiannual vibrational moaning. According to the plumber, this condition has to do with drastic changes in temperature; either we could pay thousands of dollars to have the pipes replaced or we could put up with a little annoying moaning once in awhile.

With my sister's windows closed it sounds like someone crying in the hallway at the top of the stairs. My parents, with extra years of practice under their belts, have learned to sleep through it.

Simone and I are actually engaged in something that resembles conversation. Naturally, we are talking about Buckeye. If Buckeye has done nothing else, he has given us something to talk about.

For the first time in her life Simone seems to be seriously in love. She's had boyfriends before, but Simone is the type of girl who will break up with a guy because she doesn't like the way his clothes match. She's known Buckeye for all of three weeks and is already talking about names for their children. All of this without anything close to sexual contact. "Do you really think he likes me?"

This is a question I've been asked before. "Difficult to say," I tell her. In my young life I've learned the advantages of ambivalence.

Actually, I've asked Buckeye directly how he felt for my sister and this is the response I got: "I have feelings for her, feelings that could make an Eskimo sweat, but as far as feelings go, these simply aren't the right kind. There's a control problem I'm worried about."

"He truly loves the Lord," Simone says into the night. My sister, who wouldn't know a Bible from the menu at Denny's, thinks this is beautiful.

Over the past couple of weeks I've begun to see the struggle that is going on with Buckeye, in which the Lord is surely involved. Buckeye never says anything about it, never lets on, but it's there. It's a battle that pits Buckeye the Badger against Buckeye the Mormon. Buckeye told me that in his old life as the Badger he never stole anything, never lied without first making sure he didn't have a choice, got drunk once in awhile, fought some, cussed quite a bit and had only the women that wanted him. Now, as a Mormon, there is a whole list of things he has to avoid including coffee, tea, sex, tobacco, swearing, and as Buckeye puts it, "anything else unbecoming that smacks of the natural man."

To increase his strength and defenses, Buckeye has taken to denying himself, testing his willpower in various ways. I've seen him go without food for two full days. While he watches TV he holds his breath for as long as he can, doesn't use the bathroom until he's within seconds of making a mess. As part of his rugby training, he bought an old tractor tire, filled it with rocks, made a rope harness for it and every morning drags it through the streets from his neighborhood to ours, which is at least three miles. When he comes inside he is covered with sweat but will not accept liquid of any kind. Before taking a shower he goes out onto the driveway and does a hundred pushups on his knuckles.

Since they've met, Buckeye has not so much as touched my sister except for some innocent hand-holding. Considering that he practically lives at our house and already seems like a brother-in-law, I find this a little weird. Buckeye and his non-contact love is making Simone deranged and I must say I'm enjoying it. The funny thing is, I think it's having the same effect on him. There are times when Buckeye, once perpetually casual as blue jeans, cannot stay in one spot for more than a few seconds. He moves around like someone worried about being picked off by a sniper. He will become suddenly emotional, worse than certain menstruating women I'm related to: pissed off one minute, joyful the next. All of this is not lost on Buckeye. In his calmer and more rational moments he has come to theorize that a bum gland somewhere in his brain is responsible.

I sit back and listen to the pipes moaning like mating animals behind the walls. Hummingbird Lane, the street I've lived on my entire life, stretches off both ways into darkness. The clouds are low and the lights of the city reflect off them, giving everything a green, murky glow. Next to me my sister is chatting with herself, talking about the intrigues of beauty school, some of the inane deeds of my parents, her feeling and plans for Buckeye.

"Do you think I should get baptized?" she says. "Do you think he'd want me to?"

I snort.

"What?" she says. "Just because you're an atheist or something."

"I'm not an atheist," I tell her. "I'm just not looking for any more burdens than I already have."

The next morning, on Sunday, Buckeye comes to our house a newly ordained elder. I come upstairs just in time to hear him explain to Simone and my parents that he has been endowed with the power to baptize, to preach the gospel, to lay on the administering of hands, to heal. It's the first time I've seen him in his Sunday clothes: striped shirt, blaring polyester tie and shoes that glitter so brightly you'd think they'd been shined by a Marine. He's wearing some kind of potent cologne that makes my eyes tear up if I get too close. Damn me if the phrase doesn't apply: Buckeye looks born again. As if he'd just been pulled from the womb and scrubbed a glowing pink.

"Gosh dang," Buckeye says, "do I feel nice."

I can handle Buckeye the Badger and Buckeye the Mormon, but Buckeye the Elder? When I think of elders I imagine bent, bearded men who are old enough to have the right to speak mysterious nonsense.

I have to admit, however, that he looks almost holy. He's on a high, he's ready to raise the dead. He puts up his dukes and performs some intricate Mohammed Ali footwork— something he does when he's feeling particularly successful. We all watch him in wonder. My parents, just back from prayer meeting themselves, look particularly awed.

After lunch, once Buckeye has left, we settle down for our "Sabbath family conversation." Usually it's not so much a conversation as it is an excuse for us to yell at each other in a constructive format. As always, my father calls the meeting to order and then my mother, who is a diabetic, begins by sighing and apologizing for the mess the house has been in for the past few weeks; her insulin intake has been adjusted and she hasn't been feeling well. This is just her way of blaming us for not helping out more. Simone breaks in and tries to defend herself by reminding everyone she's done the dishes twice this week, my father snaps at her for not letting my mother finish and things take their natural course from there. Simone whines, my mother rubs her temples, my father asks the Lord why we can't be a happy Christian family and I smirk and finish off my pistachio ice cream. Whenever Buckeye is not around, it seems, we go right back to normal.

Not only does Buckeye keep our household happy and lighthearted with his presence, but he has also avoided any religious confrontation with my folks. Buckeye is not naturally religious like my parents, and he doesn't say much at all, just goes about his business, quietly believing what the folks at the Mormon church teach him. This doesn't keep Mom and Dad from loving him more than anybody. I hope it doesn't sound too bitter of me to say he's the son they never had. Buckeye goes fishing with my father (I'm squeamish about putting live things on hooks) and is currently educating my mother on how to grow a successful vegetable garden. They believe a boy as well-mannered and decent as Buckeye could not be fooled by "those Mormons" for long. They are just biding their time until Buckeye comes to his spiritual senses. Then they will dazzle him with the special brand of truth found only in the Holton Hills Reformed Baptist Church, the church where they were not only saved, but where they met and eventually got married. They've tried to get Pastor Wild and Buckeye in the house at the same time but so far it hasn't worked out. Up until now, though, I would have to say that Buckeye has done most of the dazzling.

One of my biggest worries is that I will be sterile. I don't know why I think about this; I am young and have never come close to having a girl. About a year ago I was perusing the public library and found a book all about sterility and the affliction it causes in people's lives. The book said that for some people, it is a tragedy that transcends all others. In what seems to be some sort of fateful coincidence I went home and turned on the TV and there was Phil Donahue discussing this very topic with four very downtrodden-looking men and their unfulfilled wives. I didn't sleep that night and I worried about it for weeks. I even thought about secretly going to the doctor and having myself checked. I guess I believe my life has been just a little too tragedy-free for my own comfort.

This is what I'm thinking about with a rifle in my hands and Buckeye at my side. We are in a swamp looking for something to shoot. One of the big attractions of the Mormon church for Buckeye was that they don't have any outright prohibitions against shooting things. Buckeye has two rifles and a handgun he keeps under the front seat of his Oldsmobile. I've got a .22 (something larger might aggravate my shoulder) and Buckeye is toting some kind of high-caliber hunting rifle that he says could take the head off a rhino. My parents took Simone to a fashion show in Dallas, so today it's just me and Buckeye, out for a little manly fun.

I'm not sure, but it doesn't seem as if we're actually hunting anything special. The afternoon is sticky full of bugs and the chirping of birds tumbles down out of old moss-laden trees. A few squirrels whiz by and a thick black snake crosses our path, but Buckeye doesn't even notice. I guess if something worthwhile comes along, we'll shoot it.

I tell Buckeye about my sterility worries. He and I share secrets. I suppose this is something women do all the time, but I've never tried it with any of the few friends I have. This sterility thing is my last big one and probably the one that embarrasses me the most. When I get through the entire explanation Buckeye looks at me twice and laughs.

"You've never popped your cork with a girl?" he says. The expression on his face would lead me to believe that he finds this idea pretty incredible. I am really embarrassed now. I walk faster, tripping through the underbrush so Buckeye can't see all the blood rushing into my face. Buckeye picks up his pace and stays right with me. He says, "Being sterile would have been a blessing for me at your age. I used to lay pipe all over the place, and while nobody can be sure, there's a good chance I'm somebody's papa."

I stop and look at him. With Buckeye, it's more and more secrets all the time. A few days ago he told me that on a few nights of the year he can see the ghost of his mother.

"What do you mean, 'nobody can be sure?' " I say.

"With the kind of girls I used to do things with, nothing was certain. The only way you could get even a vague idea was to wait and see what color the kid came out to be."

There's a good chance Buckeye's the father of children he doesn't even know and I've got baseless worries about being sterile. Buckeye points his gun at a crow passing overhead. He follows it across the sky and says, "Don't get upset about that anyway. This is the modern world. You could have the most worthless sperm on record and there'd be a way to get around it. They've got drugs and lasers that can do just about anything. Like I say, a guy your age should only have worries about getting his cork popped. Your problem is you read too much."

I must have a confused look on my face because Buckeye
stops so he can explain himself. With a blunt finger he dia-
grams the path of his argument on my chest. "Now there's
having fun when you're young and aren't supposed to know
better, and then there's the time when you've got to come to
terms with things, line your ducks up in a row. You've got to
have sin before there's repentance. I should know about that.
Get it all out of you now. You're holding back for no good reason I can see. Some people hold it in until they're middle-aged
and then explode. And frankly, I believe there's nothing quite
as ugly as that."

We clamber through the brush for awhile, me trying to
reason through what I've just heard and Buckeye whistling
bluegrass tunes and aiming at trees. I haven't seen him this
relaxed in a long time. We come into a clearing where an old
car sits on its axles in a patch of undergrowth. Remarkably,
all its windows are still intact and we simply can't resist the
temptation to fill the thing full of holes. We're blazing away
at that sorry car, filled with the macho euphoria that comes
with making loud noises and destroying things, when a Ford
pickup barrels into the clearing on a dirt road just to the south
of us. A skinny old geezer with a grease-caked hat pulled
down over his eyes jumps out.

To get where we are, we had to crawl through a number of
barbed wire fences and there is not a lot of doubt we're on
somebody's land. The way the old man is walking toward us,
holding his rifle out in front of him, would suggest that he
is that somebody, and he's not happy that we're on his property. "You sons of bitches," he growls once he's within earshot.

"How do you do," Buckeye says back.

The man stops about twenty feet away from us, puts the
gun up to his shoulder and points it first at Buckeye, then at
me. I have never been on the business end of a firearm before

and the experience is definitely edifying. You get weak in the knees and take account of all the deeds of your life.

"This is it," the man says. He's so mad he's shaking. My attention never wavers from the end of that gun.

"Is there some problem we don't know about?" Buckeye says, still holding his gun in the crook of his arm. I have already dropped my weapon and am debating on whether or not to put my hands up.

"You damn shits!" the man nearly screeches. It's obvious he doesn't like the tone of Buckeye's voice. I wish Buckeye would notice this also.

"You come in here and wreck my property and shoot up my things and then give me this polite talk. I'm either going to take you to jail right now or shoot you where you stand and throw you in the river. I'm trying to decide."

This guy appears absolutely serious. He is weathered and bent and has a face full of scars; he looks capable of a list of things worse than murder. I begin to compose what I know will be a short and futile speech, something about the merits of mercy, but before I can deliver it Buckeye sighs and points his rifle at the old man.

"This is a perfect example of what my Uncle Lester Lewis, retired lieutenant colonel, likes to call 'mutually assured destruction.' He loves the idea. We can both stay or we can both go. As for myself, this is as good a time as any. I'm in the process of putting things right with my Maker. What about you?"

I watch the fire go out of the old man's eyes and his face get slack and pasty. He keeps his gun up but doesn't answer.

"Shall we put down our guns or stand here all day?" Buckeye says happily.

The man slowly backs up, keeping his gun trained on Buckeye. By the time he makes it back to his pickup, Buckeye has already lowered his gun. "I'm calling the police right now!" the man yells, his voice cracking into a whole range of different octaves. "They're going to put you shits away for good!"

Buckeye swings his gun up and shoots once over the man's head. As the pickup scrambles away over gravel and clumps of weeds, Buckeye shoots three or four times into the dirt behind it, sending up small *poofs* of dust. We watch the truck disappear into the trees and I work on getting my lungs functional again. Buckeye retrieves my gun and hands it to me. "We better get," he says.

We thrash through the trees and underbrush until we find the car. Buckeye drives the thing like he's playing a video game, flipping the gearshift and spinning the steering wheel. He works the gas and brake pedals with both feet and shouts at the narrow dirt road when it doesn't curve the way he expects. We skid off the road once in awhile, ending the life of a young tree, maybe, or putting a wheel into a ditch, but Buckeye never lets up. By the time we make it back to the highway we hear sirens.

"I guess that old cooter wasn't pulling our short and curlies," Buckeye says. He is clearly enjoying all this—his eyes are bright and a little frenzied. I have my head out the window in case I vomit.

Once we get back to civilization Buckeye slows down and we meander along like we're out to buy a carton of milk at the grocery store. The sirens have faded away and I don't even have a theory as to where we might be until Buckeye takes a shortcut between two warehouses and we end up in the parking lot of The Ranch. The place is deserted except for a rusty VW Bug.

"Never been here this early in the day, but it's got to be open," Buckeye says, still panting. I shrug, not yet feeling capable of forming words. It's three in the afternoon.

"When's the last time you had a nice cold beer?" Buckeye says a little wistfully.

"Never, really," I admit after a few seconds. What I don't admit to is that I've never even tasted any form of liquor in all my life. My parents have banned Simone and me from drinking alcohol until we reach the legal drinking age. Then, they say, we can decide for ourselves. Unlike Simone, I've never felt the need to defy my parents on this account. When I get together with my few friends we usually eat pizza and play Dungeons and Dragons. No one has ever suggested something like beer. Since I've known Buckeye, I've discovered what a sorry excuse for a teenager I am.

Buckeye shakes his head and whistles in disbelief. I guess we surprise each other. "Then let's go get you a beer," he says. "You're thirsty, aren't you? I'll settle for a Coke."

The front doors, big wooden affairs that swing both ways, are locked with a padlock and chain. Buckeye smiles at me and knocks on one of the doors. "There's got to be somebody in there. I know some of the people that work here. They'll get us set up."

Buckeye knocks for awhile longer but doesn't get any results. He peers through a window, goes back to the doors and pounds on them with both fists, producing a hollow booming noise that sounds like cannons from a distance. He kicks at the door and punches it a few times, leaving bright red circle-shaped scrapes on the tops of his knuckles.

"What is this?" he yells. "What is this? Hey!"

He throws his shoulder into the place where the doors meet. The doors buckle inward, making a metallic crunching noise, but the chain doesn't give. I try to tell Buckeye that I'm really not that thirsty, but he doesn't hear me. He hurls his body into the doors again, then stalks around and picks up a three-foot-high wooden cowboy next to the cement path that leads to the entrance. This squat, goofy-looking guy was carved out of a single block of wood and holds up a sign that says, "Come on in!" Buckeye emits a tearing groan and pitches it underhand against the door and succeeds only in breaking the cowboy's handlebar mustache. Buckeye has a kind of possessed look on his face, his eyes vacant, the cords in his neck taut like ropes. He picks the cowboy up again, readies himself for another throw, then drops it at his feet. He stares at me for a few seconds, his features falling into a vaguely pained expression, and sits down on the top step. He sets the cowboy upright and his hands tremble as he fiddles with the mustache, trying to make the broken part stay. He is red all over and sweating.

"I guess I'll have to owe you that beer," he says.

Simone, my father and I are sitting around the dinner table and staring at the food on our plates. We're all distraught; we poke at our enchiladas and don't look at each other. The past forty-eight hours have been rough on us: first, my mother's diabetic episode and now Buckeye has disappeared.

My mother is upstairs, resting. The doctors told her not to get out of bed for a week. Since yesterday morning old ladies from the church have been bringing over food, flowers and get-well cards in waves. In the kitchen we have casseroles stacked into pyramids.

As for Buckeye, nobody has seen him in two days. He hasn't called or answered his phone. My father has just returned from the boarding house where Buckeye rents a room and the owner told him that she hadn't seen Buckeye either, but it was against her policy to let strangers look in the rooms.

"One more day and we'll have to call the police," my father says. He's made this exact statement at least three times now.

Simone, distressed as she is, cannot get any food in her mouth. She looks down at the food on her plate as if it's something she can't fully comprehend. She gets a good forkful of enchiladas halfway to her mouth before she loses incentive and drops the fork back onto her plate. I think it's the first time in her twenty-one years that she's had to deal with real-life problems more serious than the loss of a contact lens.

It all started three days ago, one day after the incident with the guns. I spent that entire morning nursing an irrational fear that somehow the police were going to track us down and there would be a patrol car pulling up outside the house any minute. I was the only one home except for my mother, who had taken the day off sick from work and was sleeping upstairs.

I holed myself up in my basement bedroom to watch TV and read my books. At about four o'clock I heard a knock at the front door and nearly passed out from fright. I had read in magazines what happens in prisons to young clean people like me. I was sure that trespassing and destruction of property, not to mention shooting in the general direction of the owner, would get Buckeye and me some serious time in the pen.

The knocking came again and then someone opened the front door. I pictured a police officer coming in our house with his pistol drawn. I turned off the light in my room, hid myself in the closet, and listened to the footsteps upstairs. It took me only a few seconds to recognize the heavy shuffling gait of Buckeye.

Feeling relieved and a little ridiculous, I ran upstairs to find Buckeye going down the hall toward my parents' room.

"Hey, bubba," he said when he saw me. "Nobody answered the door so I let myself in. Simone told me your mother's sick. I've got something for her." He held up a mason jar filled with a dark green substance.

"She's just tired," I said. "What is that?"

"It's got vitamins and minerals," he said. "Best thing in the world for sick and tired people. My grandpop taught me how to make it. All natural, no artificial flavors or colors although it could probably use some. It smells like what you might find in a baby's diaper and doesn't taste much better."

"Mom's sleeping," I said. "She told me not to wake her up unless there was an emergency."

"How long's she been asleep?" Buckeye said.

"Pretty much the whole day," I told him.

Buckeye looked at his watch. "That's not good. She needs to have something to eat. Nutrients and things."

I shrugged and Buckeye shrugged back. He looked worried and a little run-down himself. His hair flopped aimlessly around on his head. He rubbed the jar in his hands like it was a magic lamp.

"You could leave it and I'll give it to her. Or you can wait until she wakes up. Simone will be home pretty soon."

Buckeye looked at me and weighed his options. Then he turned on his heels, walked right up to my parents' bedroom door and rapped on it firmly. I deserted the hallway for the kitchen, not wanting to be implicated in this in any way. I was there only a few seconds when Buckeye appeared, short of breath and a peaked look on his face.

"Something's wrong," he said. "Your mother."

My mother was lying still on the bed, her eyes open, unblinking, staring at nothing. Her skin was pale and glossy and her swollen tongue was hanging out of her mouth and covered with white splotches. I stood in the doorway while Buckeye telephoned an ambulance. "Mama?" I called from where I was standing. For some reason I couldn't make myself go any closer.

I walked out into the front yard and nearly fell on my face.

Everything went black for a moment. I thought I'd gone blind. When my sight came back the world looked so sharp and real it hurt. I picked up a rock from the flower planter and chucked it at the Conley's big bay window across the street. I guess I figured that if my mother was dead, no one could blame me for doing something like that. I had always felt a special distaste for Mr. Conley and his fat sweating wife. I missed the window and the rock made a hollow thump on the fiberglass siding of the house. I cursed my uncoordinated body. If I had played Little League like my father had wanted all those years ago, that window would have been history.

I reeled around in the front yard until my father and the ambulance showed up. My mind didn't want to approach the idea that my mother might be lying deceased in her bed, so I didn't go near the house to find out. I hung out in the corner of the yard and swung dangerously back and forth in the lilac bushes. I watched the ambulance pull up and the paramedics run into my house followed a few minutes later by my father, who didn't even look my way. Neighbors were beginning to appear. I noticed their bald and liver-spotted heads poking out of windows and screen doors.

After a little while my father came out and found me sitting in the gardenias. He told me that my mother was not dead, but that she had had a severe diabetic reaction. "Too much insulin, not enough food," he said, wiping his eyes. "Why doesn't she take care of herself?"

I'd seen my mother have minor reactions, when she would get numb all over and forget what her name was and we'd have to make her eat candy or drink soda until she became better, but nothing like this. My father put his hand on my back and guided me inside where the paramedics were strapping her onto a stretcher. She didn't look any better than before.

"She's not dead," I said. I was honestly having trouble believing my father. I thought he might be trying to pull a fast one on me, saving me from immediate grief and shock. To me, my mother looked as dead as anything I'd ever seen, as dead as my aunt Sally in her coffin a few years ago, dense and filmy, like a figure carved from wax.

My father looked at me, his eyes moist and drawn, and shook his head. "She's serious, Lord help her, but she'll make it," he said. "I'm going to the hospital with her. I'll call you when I get there. Go and pray for her. That's what she needs from you."

I watched them load her into the ambulance and then went upstairs to pray. I had never really prayed in all my life, though I'd mouthed the words in Sunday school. But my father said that was what my mother needed, and helpless and lost as I felt, I couldn't come up with anything better to do.

I found Buckeye in my sister's room kneeling at the side of the bed. My first irrational thought was that he might be doing something questionable in there, looking through her underwear, etc., but then he started speaking and there was no doubt that I was listening to a prayer. He had his face pushed into his hands but his voice came at me as if he were talking to me through a pipe. I can't remember a word he said, only that he pleaded for my mother's life and health in a way that made it impossible for me to move away from the door and leave him to his privacy. I forgot myself completely and stood dumbly above the stairs, my hand resting on the doorknob.

Buckeye rocked on his knees and talked to the Lord. If it is possible to be humble and demanding at the same time, Buckeye was pulling it off: he dug the heels of his hands into his forehead and called on the Almighty in a near shout. He asked questions and seemed to get answers. He pleaded for mercy. He chattered on for minutes, lost in something that seemed to range from elation to despair. I have never heard anything like that, never felt that way before. Light was going up and down my spine and hitting the backs of my eyes. I don't think it's stretching it to say that for a few moments, I was genuinely certain that God, who or whatever He may be, was in that room. Despite myself, I had to peek around the door to make sure there was really nobody in there except Buckeye.

After Buckeye finished, I stumbled into my parents' room and sat on their bed. I put my hand on the place my mother's body had made an indentation in the sheets and picked the hairs off her pillow. Buckeye's prayer had been enough; I didn't think I could add much more. I sat there and mumbled aloud to no one in particular that I backed up everything Buckeye had said, one hundred percent.

We went to the hospital and after an eternity of reading women's magazines and listening to Simone's sobbing, a doctor came out and told us that it looked like my mother would be fine, that we were lucky we found her when we did because if we had let her sleep another half hour she certainly wouldn't have made it. Simone began to sob even louder and I looked at Buckeye, but he didn't react to what the doctor said. He slumped in his chair and looked terribly tired. Relief sucked everything out of me and left me so weak that I couldn't help but let loose a few stray tears myself.

While my father filled out insurance forms, Buckeye mumbled something about needing to get some sleep. He gave Simone a kiss on the forehead and patted my father and me on the back and wandered away into the dark halls of the hospital. That was the last any of us saw of him.

My mother's nearly buying the farm and the disappearance of Buckeye, the family hero, has thrown us all into a state. I poke at a mound of Jell-O with my fork and say, "I bet he's just had a good run of luck selling pantyhose. By now he's probably selling them to squaws in Oklahoma." I don't really know why I say things like this. I guess it's because I'm the baby of the family, a teenager, and making flippant, smart-ass remarks is part of my job.

My father shakes his head in resigned paternal disappointment and Simone bares her teeth and throws me a look of such hate that I'm unable to make another comment. My father asks me why I don't go to my room and do something worthwhile. I decide to take his advice. Simone looks like she's meditating violence. I thump down the stairs, turn up my stereo as loud as it will go, lie down on my bed and stare at the ceiling. Before I go to sleep I imagine sending words to heaven, having the clouds open up before me, revealing a light so brilliant I can't make out what's inside.

I'm awakened by a sound like a manhole cover being slid from its place. It's dark in my room, the music is off and someone has put a blanket over me. Most likely my father, who occasionally acts quite motherly when my mother is not able to. There is a scrape and a thud and I twist around to see Buckeye stuffed into the small window well on the other side of the room, looking at me through the glass.

He has pushed away the wrought-iron grate that covers the well and is squatting in the dead leaves and spider webs that cover the bottom of it. Buckeye is just a big jumble of shadow and moonlight, but I can still make out his unmistakable smile. I get up and slide open the window.

"Good evening," Buckeye whispers, polite as ever. He presses his palms against the screen. "I didn't want to wake you up, but I brought you something. Do you want to come out here?"

I run upstairs, go out the front door and find Buckeye trying to lift himself out of the window well onto the grass. I help
him up and say, "Where have you been?"

When Buckeye straightens up and faces me, I get a strong
whiff of alcohol and old sweat. He acts like he didn't hear my
question. He holds up a finger, indicating for me to wait a
moment, and goes to his car, leaning to the right just a little.
He comes back with a case of Stroh's and bestows it on me as
if it's a red pillow with the crown jewels on top. "This is that
beer I owe you," he says, his voice gritty and raw with drink.
"I wanted to get you a keg of the good-tasting stuff, but I
couldn't find any this late."

We stand in the wet grass and look at each other. His lower
lip is split and swollen, his half-ear is a mottled purple and he's
got what looks like lipstick smudged on his chin. His boots are
muddy and he's wearing the same clothes he had on three
days ago.

"Your mother okay?" he says.

"She's fine. They want her to stay in bed a week or so."

"Simone?"

"She's been crying a lot."

For a long time he just stands there, his face gone slack, and
looks past me to the dark house. "Everybody asleep in there?"

I look at my watch. It's almost three-thirty in the morning.
"I guess so," I say.

Buckeye says, "Hey, let's take a load off. Looks like you're
about to drop that beer." We walk over to the porch and sit
down on the front steps. I keep the case in my lap, not really
knowing what to do with it. Buckeye pulls off two cans, pops
them open, hands one to me.

I have the first beer of my life sitting on our front porch
with Buckeye. It's warm and sour but not too bad. I feel
strange, like I haven't completely come out of sleep. I have so

many questions looping through my brain that I can't con-
centrate on one long enough to ask it. Buckeye takes a big
breath and looks down into his hands. "What can I say?" he
whispers. "I thought I was getting along fine and the next
thing I know I'm face down in the dirt, right back where I
started from. I can't remember much, but I just let loose. I lost
my strength for just a minute and that's all it takes. For awhile
there I didn't even want to behave." He gets up, walks out to
the willow tree and touches its leaves with his fingers, comes
back to sit down. "I think I got ahead of myself. This time I've
got to take things slower."

"Are you going somewhere?" I ask. It seems to be the only
question that means anything right now.

"I don't know. I'll keep looking for Bud. He's the only
brother I've got that I'm aware of. I've just got to get away,
start things over again."

Not having anything to say, I nod. We have a couple more
beers together and stare into the distance. I want to tell
Buckeye about hearing him pray for my mother, thinking
it might change something, but I can't coax out the words.
Finally, Buckeye stands up and whacks some imaginary dust
from his pants. "I'd leave a note for Simone and your folks
. . . ," he says.

"I'll tell them," I say.

"Lord," Buckeye says. "Damn."

He sticks his big hand out for a shake, a habit he picked up
from the Mormons, and gives me a knuckle-popping squeeze.
As he walks away on the cement path toward his car, the
inside of my chest feels as big as a room and I have an over-
powering desire to tackle him, take his legs out, pay him back
for my collarbone, hold him down and tell him what a god-
damned bastard I think he is. This feeling stays with me for
all of five seconds, then bottoms out and leaves me as I was

before, the owner of one long list of emotions: sorry that it had to turn out this way for everybody; relieved that Buckeye is back to his natural self; pleased that he came to see me before he left; afraid of what life will be like without having him around.

Buckeye starts up his battle wagon and instead of just driving slowly away into the distance, which would probably be the appropriate thing to do under these circumstances, he gets the car going in a tight circle, four, five times around in the middle of the quiet street, muffler rattling, tires squealing and bumping the curb, horn blowing, a hubcap flying into somebody's yard—all for my benefit.

I go into the house before the last rumbles of Buckeye's car die away. I take my case of beer and hide it under my bed, already planning the hell-raising beer party I'll have with some of my friends. I figure it's about time we did something like that. On the way down the stairs, I wobble a little and bump into things, feeling like the whole house is pitching beneath my feet. All at once it hits me that I'm officially roasted. Gratified, I go back upstairs and into my father's den where he keeps the typewriter I've never seen him use.

I feed some paper into the dusty old machine and begin typing. I've decided not to tell anyone about Buckeye's last visit; it will be the final secret between us. Instead, I go to work composing the letter Buckeye would certainly have left had he learned to write. I address it to Simone and just let things flow. I don't really try to imitate Buckeye's voice, but somehow I can feel it coming out in a crusty kind of eloquence. Even though I've always been someone who's highly aware of grammar and punctuation, I let sentence after sentence go by without employing so much as a comma. I tell Simone everything Buckeye could have felt and then some. I tell her how much she means to me and always will. I tell her what a peach she is. I'm shameless, really. I include my parents and thank them for everything, inform them that as far as I'm concerned, no two more Christian people ever walked the earth. I philosophize about goodness and badness and the sweet sorrow of parting. As I type, I imagine my family reading this at the breakfast table and the heartache compressing their faces, emotion rising in them so full that they are choked into speechlessness. This image spurs me on and I clack away on the keys like a single-minded idiot. When I'm finished, I've got two and a half pages and nothing left to say. A little stunned, I sit in my father's chair and strain in the dim light to see what I've just written. Until now, I've never been aware of what being drunk can do for one's writing ability.

I take the letter out on the front porch and tack it to our front door, feeling ridiculously like Martin Luther, charged with conviction and fear. I go back inside and try to go to sleep but I'm restless—the blood inside me is hammering against my ribs and the ends of my fingers, the house is too dark and cramped. Instead of going up the stairs, I push out my window screen and climb out the well and begin to run around the house, the sun a little higher in the sky every time I come around into the front yard. I feel light-headed and weightless and I run until my lungs are raw, trying to get the alcohol out of my veins before my parents wake up.

Ballad of
the Ball and Chain

———————————○———————————

I couldn't deny it anymore: Juan, the man in my life, was out of his mind. Whacked-out, loony, apeshit—pick a word, they all describe the person Juan had become. I'd tried to convince myself that he just needed time to adjust, pull together, come to terms, but I had to face the sad truth—if anything, he was getting worse. He refused to get professional help, so all I could do was tell him that I loved him and keep him out of public view.

My friends at work told me I was overreacting. He's healthy, isn't he? they would say. He's not on drugs or violent or anything, right? These things take *time*, they would say, as if they understood the situation perfectly.

The thing is, I never told them the whole story. I said that

Juan was acting strangely and left it pretty much at that. They were not aware that it had been at least two months since he had laid a comb or brush to his hair. They hadn't seen the flat look in his eyes or the terrible hat he wore all the time. They hadn't watched him, as I had, wad up a piece of aluminum foil and chew on it until tears came to his eyes. They didn't know how terrified I was that he was going to stay this way forever.

All of this started on a spring night as beautiful as any other here in Cedar City, Utah. It was the bachelor party for Bart Givens, Juan's lifelong best friend. They went to school together, were the famed double-play combo on the state champion baseball team. They spent so much time together, were so close, there had been rumors floating around town for years that they were lovers. Even though they were not related in any way, they looked like twins with their bleach-bottle-blond hair, wide shoulders and Hollywood smiles.

Bart was to be married the next afternoon to a girl he had met on one of his sales trips to Salt Lake, a radio weather person named Kitty Logan. Juan was to be the best man. He already had his tuxedo—a tasteless maroon get-up with a mint-green cummerbund—laid out over a chair in our bedroom, ready for the big ceremony.

The party was held right here in our house. Imagine the most depraved sort of gathering that could be put together by a bunch of shameless yahoos and there you have it: piles of buffalo wings, beer flowing from kegs, old-fashioned black-and-white porno flicks playing on the wall, a belly-dancer with hand-clappers and with tiny brass saucers glued to her nipples. Juan and I agreed it would not be a good idea for me to be present for such a spectacle, so I went across the street to Mrs. Whetstone's where I could still keep an eye on things. It was a warm night and the windows and doors were flung open so I could pretty much see and hear everything. From the shadows of Mrs. Whetstone's porch, I watched these men, all respectable citizens by day—lawyers and salesmen and schoolteachers—groping after the juking belly dancer, making obscene gestures involving their hips and tongues, belching and vomiting and yelling at each other over the thumping music. Every once in awhile I'd walk across the street and stand on the lawn where I could get a better vantage point. No one noticed me; they were all too busy letting themselves go.

After everything settled down, after the belly dancer had escaped and the beer had run its course, Juan brought out what he was sure would be the event of the evening: a four-foot chain welded on one end to a manacle and on the other to a genuine Civil War cannon ball he had bought from Harris Dinty, an old junk-metal collector who lived just south of town. Juan had spent a week at the high school metal shop manufacturing it. When he finished the welding, he sanded the rust off and painted the whole contraption with a high-gloss black paint, polishing it until he could see his own warped reflection.

The whole group of them grinning like imbeciles, they waylaid Bart, held him down and padlocked the ball and chain to his left ankle. Juan made a speech about how the ball and chain was representative of the institution of marriage and that its purpose was, from now until the wedding, to remind Bart that as of five o'clock tomorrow afternoon he would be giving up his freedom, his life savings, his privacy, his comfort and carefree attitude, his optimistic world view. Hopefully, he said, looking Bart straight in the eye, it will make you think twice. There is still time, somebody said. All the married men in attendance nodded their heads gravely. Someone who was sprawled out of sight behind the couch began to croon a broken version of "Ballad of the Ball and Chain." Bart held the ball in his lap, stroking it, and said, "I love this thing."

I watched them leave, stumbling out across the lawn to their cars. Bart was the last one, leaning forward with the chain in his hand, dragging the ball behind him like a baby with a wet blanket. He sped off in his convertible and Juan stood out in the grass, waving happily and shouting, "Think twice, you fucker!"

I went home, put Juan to bed, and began cleaning up. It was four a.m., I was just finishing and ready to go to bed myself, when the phone rang. It was Sheriff Ralsy telling me in modulated tones that they had found Bart Givens at the bottom of the reservoir, drowned. Apparently he'd fallen asleep at the wheel and plunged into the north end, near the dock. He was driving a convertible, the reservoir was no more than twelve feet deep and he would have had no trouble at all swimming his way to safety had he not been weighed down by a ball and chain padlocked to his leg.

I laughed right then, God help me, I giggled out loud. It was four in the morning, I had just witnessed the love of my life sponsor an evening of orchestrated depravity, and now here was the sheriff, in his textbook sheriff's voice, telling me this.

I woke Juan up and put the phone to his ear, which was smeared purple with the belly dancer's lipstick. I watched his face collapse as he listened to the news, watched his eyes roll in his head as if searching for somewhere to hide, heard him whimper a few confused vowels, and when he hung up, I hugged him. Seeing him like this, whatever urge I'd felt to laugh at the absurdity of this situation was gone. Juan leaned into me, mashing his face into my collarbone until thick, hoarse groans—*oh, oh, oh, oh, oh*—came tearing out of him.

He clenched my hair with one hand and pounded me on the back with the other so hard it left bruises.

The only good thing that came out of this whole mess was that Juan stopped smoking. I don't know why. After that night, as far as I know, he never touched a cigarette. No more drinking, either. I would still find packets of Lucky Strikes hidden in places all over the house, stashed in case he ever ran out. I always hated Juan's smoking and now that the house was finally starting to smell okay again, I found myself wishing for that stale sour scent, for the smoke drifting up and pooling in the corners of the ceilings, the heaps of bent butts in ashtrays. For months, half a keg of sour beer sat like a squat, accusing Buddha on top of our fridge.

For the first few nights after the accident Juan made the pretense of getting in bed with me, but he never came close to sleep. One of those nights, I remember him tossing and sighing and kicking off the covers and pulling them up again. Finally he jumped out of bed and ran out of the room. I heard him throwing things around in the pantry, then going out the back door. I got up and looked out the window and there he was in the back yard, bare-skinned except for his milky white Fruit of the Looms glowing in the moonlight. His face shadowed and sinister, he was beating the bushes with a whining Dustbuster in his hand, muttering, "Where are you, fucking cricket."

After that night he didn't bother getting into bed with me at all. Instead, he would wander the house like a ghost. At night, he said, he could hear everything: mice running in the walls, the buzz of telephone wires, satellites beeping overhead, all the desert animals skittering over the sand. He told me that only in the day, when there were enough sounds to cancel each other out, could he find the sleep he needed.

And then there was the hat. I came home from work one day and found him in the tub with no water in it, a bottle of Southern Comfort in his hand and a green fedora on his head. The hat was the kind of thing a senior citizen would wear to play bingo or watch the dog races—it had a blue satin band and a red wispy feather that looked like it might have come from a very old and unhealthy bird. The kind of hat no one under seventy-five would be caught dead wearing.

"I'm not going to drink this stuff," he said, holding out the bottle. "I've just got it to look at."

"It doesn't fit," I said.

"What?"

"The hat—too small."

"I found it, Rita."

"Where?"

"Bart's garage."

It was the longest conversation we'd had in a week. I decided I'd press my luck.

"Your boss called this morning. He says your vacation and sick leave are finished day after tomorrow. He says he understands what you're going through but he wanted to know if he should start looking for a replacement."

I wanted Juan to react, to address his troubles or make excuses, anything, but he just smiled, his eyes sad, and leaned back in the tub as if he was floating in a cloud of Mr. Bubble. He wouldn't talk to me for the rest of the day.

None of this, though—the not speaking, the not sleeping, the hat—bothered me as much as when he tried to hurt himself. The time I caught him chewing on tin foil I asked him what he was doing and he told me, "I want to hurt."

"No you don't," I said.

"Yes I do. It's the only thing that makes me feel better."

"You hurt enough already."

"No, no—hah!—no." He shook his head. "Not near enough."

He would do the dishes with the water scalding. Some mornings he would sit at the kitchen table with his old Algebra II book, the same one he was never able to decipher in high school, and attempt to find the solutions, the answers to all the problems, gnashing his teeth, sometimes crying in frustration. "This is not right," he'd weep. "The answers in the back of the book are all screwed up. Somebody should definitely do something about this."

He rubbed bacon on his arm and tried to get Louise, my retriever, to bite him. Sometimes he would run out into the desert at night, barefoot, over the rocks and bullheads and clumps of sagebrush, trying to sneak up on coyotes. I remember him once or twice calling the police, asking them to come over and arrest him.

He began to wear that damn hat everywhere. It seemed to give him the kind of comfort that I couldn't.

Juan and I met in the Green River, a year and a half before the accident. He was ankle deep in the water, serenely peeing into the current, and I was about twenty yards upstream, soaking my legs after a long day of hiking, partly hidden by some cattails. When he noticed me, he just finished his business, stuffed his thing back in his spandex biking shorts and waded over to introduce himself. Here was this blond, tiger-eyed man standing above me, shirtless and dripping sweat, the sun like a corona behind his head. I think it was when he told me his name was Juan that I began to truly love him.

I had just spent two years in eastern Wyoming doing grasslands research, and my social skills, never my strong point anyway, had devolved into a limited repertoire of grunts and head movements that I utilized mostly in refusing offers to dance from cowboys and truck drivers. I told Juan my name but couldn't come up with anything else. I felt ridiculous, but there was nothing left to do but tell him exactly what I was thinking: "You are one beautiful man."

He looked over his shoulder and back at me. "I hope that has nothing to do with what you just saw me doing over there," he said.

I asked him about his name and he told me he was named after Juan María Batista, a Mexican revolutionary around the turn of the century who fought against the aristocracy, a liberator of the oppressed and champion of the poor. He squatted down in the water next to me to explain all this, his knee touching my elbow, and I have never been so turned on in all my life.

We started going out and six months later we moved in together. Originally, I had come to Cedar City to finish up my graduate work in Land Management, but meeting Juan made me lose my concentration, my devotion to scientific analysis. We ripped up the front lawn and planted a pumpkin garden, we drove out to Shipwreck Rock and made love on building-sized slabs of sandstone, we brewed dandelion wine that tasted like bleach. I knew we were acting like hormone-driven teenagers, but I didn't care; I was so happy, so *full*. Even though I'd grown up dreaming about delirious, headlong romance, I'd never even had a boyfriend, not even in high school, and I had eventually resigned myself to a solitary existence. But now, here was Juan, like a last-minute miracle, a gift of God fallen from the sky; I had found someone to love.

I got a job showing sun-drunk tourists around rock formations and Indian ruins. Juan, who was born and raised in Cedar City, already had a good job at the biggest insurance company in town, but drove around in a rusty Maverick and was always borrowing money from Bart. It took him two or three weeks after we'd moved in together to tell me why.

It happened on a Saturday morning when we were out biking, coasting down a narrow canyon trail. I started yammer-
ing about marriage, asking his opinions on the role of
husband and wife in this day and age, etc. It was not something that had ever come up between us, and I was curious to
know what he thought. I did not mean anything by it, so far
as I know, had absolutely no hidden intentions, but Juan suddenly stopped his bike, actually stuck out his heels and
skidded to a stop instead of applying the hand brake.

"Whoa," he said. "Hold on just a second here."

I sped a good ten yards past him and had to turn around
and go back. He was gripping the handle bars. His ears
were suddenly red. He stared at one spot in the middle of
his chest—something he does when he's thinking, gathering words, preparing to speak. He unstraddled his bike and
tossed it aside as if it was hindering his thought processes.
He walked to the other side of the trail, kicked at a dead
yucca plant and came back talking: "I've got something to
tell you and it's not a secret or anything like that, just something I haven't said anything about until now. I don't believe
in secrets."

He looked up for the first time and I tried to affect an
expression of openness, acceptance, an expression that said,
Tell me what you must.

"I have an ex-wife," he said.

"What?"

"And a kid."

My bike tipped over and slid down a shallow embankment,
hitting a boulder.

"All right," he said, putting his hands out in front of him as
if clearing the air. "I'm just going to get all this out right now
and then we won't have to talk about it again. Okay?"

Unable to speak at all, I nodded.

"Seven years," he said, stopped, sighed, put his hands over his eyes and started again: "Seven years ago I got married. I saw this girl in her tight jeans and cowboy boots and I thought we had a date with destiny. And then, *ka-pow*"—he punched himself fairly hard on the side of the head—"here comes a baby before I can even get my legs under me. I was a freshman in college for godssakes, weak in the knees to begin with. I was afraid of the baby. Of what it might grow up to be under the care of a moron like me. I was afraid of the way Carolyn was always looking at me, begging me to take charge. It was pure hell, every day of it. Torture. It took her two years to get up enough sense to leave, take the baby and clear out. She moved to Virginia Beach and started a T-shirt shop. She's happy, far as I know. My alimony and child support don't hurt, either."

"You have a child," I said.

"Gordon. He's not a bad soccer player, from what I hear. I'm supposed to have visitation rights, but she moved as far away from me as she could get. It's better this way. Except for those checks I send out every month, it's like something that never happened." He rubbed the sweat off his neck and smoothed his long hair back with it. "I don't know what else to say."

"I'm sorry," I said.

"About what?"

"I don't know, all this," I said. I felt terribly strange right then; in a matter of seconds Juan had become someone completely different to me, a whole different person. He suddenly seemed older and more vulnerable, which, for some reason, made me love him even more.

"Look," he said. "This isn't a confession or anything terrible like that. You started talking about marriage and everything—it's just I want you to know how I feel about it, the

whys and the wherefores. Marriage, in my opinion, is the
worst damn idea anybody ever came up with. If we stopped
and thought logically about it, we'd ban the whole thing.
What's the purpose in it? Shouldn't we be free to love each
other and not be obligated?"

Juan—quiet, untalkative Juan—was running at the mouth
and he knew it. He gathered me into his arms and hugged me
as if to stop himself from going on.

"I'm happy, the way we are," he said into my hair.

I squeezed him as hard as I could, until I heard his ribs
creak.

"Exactly," he said, as if I had just agreed with him.

I found out during those months after the accident—months
of sick worry and heartache and crying alone in bed—that
there is nothing more cruel than hope. I believed that if I
simply loved Juan enough—no matter that he had become a
whole different person, a shabby refugee from some unnam-
able place—he would come out of it, suddenly or gradually,
and we would be able to start our perfect life all over again. I
believed in this, clung to this hope, even while I held Juan
down in the bath tub and scrubbed the grit off him, like a dog,
even when I'd have to wake up every hour or two in the middle of the night to check in on him, to make sure he wasn't
hurting himself in any permanent way, even during the long
days of telephone calls from newspaper and TV people, wanting to do interviews, wanting to know about this wacky mis-
adventure with a ball and chain that had ended in watery
death.

I think I held up well, all things considered, until one
morning, just under six months after the accident, when I got
out of bed and found that Juan had disappeared. I tore
through the house in a red-eyed panic, checked the garage,

the attic, the backyard, shouting Juan's name. Before, I had convinced myself that I shouldn't worry about suicide, that Juan wasn't capable of such a thing, but now it was the only thing in my head; my mind was a huge movie screen full of all the gory, self-inflicted possibilities.

In nothing more than a long T-shirt I got in my car and searched every street in town, the park, I even went out to the reservoir, thinking that might be the place Juan might choose to do something drastic. Once I had scoured the entire area I sped home to call the sheriff to start a manhunt. I came screeching into the driveway and when I got out of the car I looked up and there was Juan sitting on the roof. I stood there for a moment, half-naked, my breath coming in jerks, staring up at him. He was sitting with his back against the chimney, eyes closed, wearing a pair of flowery swim trunks and his hat. The sun made a halo around his head, just as it had the first day we met.

"Have you been up there this whole time?" I yelled at him. Juan didn't acknowledge my presence; I knew he had been perched up there while I shouted his name and ripped the house apart looking for him. He must have just sat and watched while I tore out of the driveway, hysterical and nauseous with dread.

"What are you doing up there?" I said.

He said, "Getting sunburned."

"Will you come down? Please."

Without even looking my way he said, "Don't you have work today?"

Something broke inside me right then; the tide of panic that had overtaken me turned, almost instantly, into an anger so deep and complete that I could feel my entire body begin to shake. The relief I'd felt at finding him safe and sound was completely washed away. I wanted to throw rocks at Juan, I wanted to hurt him, I wanted to give him some of that pain he was searching for.

"You son of a BITCH!" I shrieked.

Juan didn't say anything, but I thought I could see him smile ever so slightly.

I went inside and tried to calm myself, standing just inside the door, taking deep breaths, my face pressed against the wall. I found my way to the kitchen and called the tourist office to tell them I wouldn't be able to make the Red Canyon tour because I had the flu. Julie, my supervisor, swore and hung up on me. I didn't hang up the phone, just disconnected and dialed again—9-1-1.

"Emergency services," the man on the other end said. He sounded much too cheerful to be doing the job he was doing.

"I need help," I said.

"What's your address, please, ma'am."

I told him and then explained that there was somebody on my roof.

"What is this person doing there?"

"Just sitting."

"Is this person an acquaintance or family member?"

"No—sort of."

"You can tell me."

"He's just someone I know and I don't want him to fall and hurt himself. Maybe you could send someone over to talk to him. Nothing I do seems to work."

"Has he been taking drugs or alcohol?

"No, no."

"Does he have a history of mental illness?"

"Not really."

"Is he in possession of any kind of weapon or firearm?"

"No, look, it's no big deal. I just wanted to talk to somebody, I'm sorry to bother you."

"Please stay on the line, ma'am, I can't help you if you hang up."

"Thanks, really, but—"

Just then there was a loud scraping noise and a series of thumps right above my head. Through the sliding glass door I saw Juan come hurtling off the roof, like a piece of space debris falling out of the sky, landing without a sound on the grass of the backyard.

"I heard that," the man on the phone said.

I hung up and went to the back door. Juan slowly picked himself up off the lawn. Dazed, he stumbled in a circle, clutching the air for something to steady himself with. He looked around until he found his hat in a bush and clapped it on his head. He had at least three nasty scrapes on his shoulder and back.

I slid open the door and he looked at me. I could now see that his left hand was sticking out from his wrist at a sickeningly unnatural angle. He suddenly grabbed his arm and winced. "I think I fell asleep up there," he said.

I went to him, but he held out his good hand, stopping me. "I'm okay," he said, unable to stop flinching as he tried to move his arm. "I'm not feeling too bad at all."

We were back from the hospital only a few minutes when Kitty Logan, Bart's ex-fiancee, called. I was sitting at the kitchen table, feeling so exhausted that it took everything I had just to get up and answer the phone, and Juan was curled up under the sink, snoring lightly while Louise licked his toes. The hospital had been an ordeal: Juan fought the paramedics the whole way there, fought the nurses and doctors in the hallway of the emergency room, shouting defiantly, like a wild-eyed political dissident, that he didn't have a broken bone, he didn't want any help from anybody, and finally it took a three-hundred pound janitor to hold Juan down long enough so they could give him a sedative and work on his broken wrist.

When I finally made it to the phone, Kitty, in her polished radio voice, told me that she was on her way to Phoenix and she wanted to drop by if that was all right with us. She'd heard through the grapevine that Juan wasn't taking the whole thing so well and she wanted to stop by and assure him that she had no hard feelings, that it had just been one of those freak things that no one could be blamed for. I left her on the line to ask Juan what he thought. When I told him Kitty was on the phone, he sat up and hit his head on the drain pipe—a reverberating *kronk* that made Louise whine. He crawled out from under the sink and when I told him Kitty wanted to visit he swayed sideways as if caught by a sudden wind.

"Is it all right?" I said. "Do you want to see her?"

Juan grabbed the kitchen table for balance and held on. He didn't seem to notice the bone-white cast he was now wearing.

"Juan?" I said.

"Kitty," Juan said.

"He'd love to see you," I said into the phone. "We both would."

Two hours later, at exactly seven o'clock, Kitty showed up at the front door, just as she said she would. Juan was still in the bathroom doing Lord-knows-what—rifling through drawers, running the water, banging the toilet seat up and down.

I let Kitty in and offered her something to drink. She was a pretty woman, the kind of woman that can wear purple lipstick and hoop earrings and not look like a slut. She and I had met only once before, up in Salt Lake, a few weeks before the planned wedding. We all went to a movie and she and I might have become better acquainted that night had she and

Bart been able to extricate their hands and faces from one another for a few minutes.

I got her some cranberry juice and asked her how she was holding up.

She shrugged and smiled at me—a smile without a trace of grief or bitterness in it. "Pretty good, really. I cried a lot those first few days, but I've pretty much accepted that this is the way things were supposed to happen."

I nodded, doing my best to keep my smile as genuine as hers.

"Hmm," she said, looking down at her drink.

"Juan, Kitty's here," I called over my shoulder.

Juan came out of the bathroom wearing his hat and an old plaid blazer I'd never seen before. With his hair slicked back over his ears and his puffy, sunburned face, he looked like a homeless man going to interview for a fast-food job. He shuffled into the room staring at his shoes.

"Juan?" Kitty said, then glanced over at me to verify that this really was not some heat-weary vagrant off the street.

"He's had a tough time," I said.

Juan raised his head, holding out his hands as if he had given up searching for something he'd lost. "Kitty," he said. "Holy shit." The look in his eyes was enough to break my heart.

Kitty got up and put her hand on Juan's shoulder. "Let's just talk about this. Will you sit next to me here?" She tried to lead him over to the couch but he tilted his head apologetically, resisting her, staying where he was.

"Juan," she said. "You have to get over this. Life goes on. It's nobody's fault."

"Yes," Juan said. "*C'est la vie*."

"It just takes time."

Juan said, "I'm sorry I didn't go to the funeral. I'm a serious piece of shit."

I cut in. "The doctors gave him tranquilizers that made him sick. I made him stay home."

"No, no," Kitty said, holding her hands in front of her. "I understand completely."

After a moment he said to Kitty, "Can you do me a favor?"

"Name it," she said.

Juan turned around and went to the hall closet. He came back with an aluminum baseball bat. He held it out to her and said, "I heard you're quite a softball player. Bart used to tell me that you had a hell of a major league swing. He said with genes like that he was sure you two could raise up the next Mickey Mantle."

He held the bat out in front of him until Kitty accepted it. "Will you do something for me?" he asked her.

Unsure, Kitty nodded.

Juan tapped his left temple and said, "Just give me a solid one right here." He stepped forward a little, stretching his neck out so his head was within range.

Kitty made a little half-laugh, half-gasp and looked over at me for help.

"Batter up," Juan said.

"Juan," I said.

Juan looked at her with the sorrowful calm of a lame horse waiting to be shot. Kitty seemed to be hyperventilating and I couldn't tell if she was terrified or angry or both.

"It would help a lot," Juan whispered.

Kitty began crying but she would not put down the bat. Not taking her eyes off Juan's shining forehead, she began to cock the bat behind her ear. I went over and took it away from her. "Oh Lord," she sobbed, covering her mouth, gathering her purse, moving toward the door.

"I'm sorry," I said.

"It's nothing," Kitty said, her cheeks slick with tears, her hands fluttering around her like broken-backed birds.

"You'd be surprised at the amount of trauma the human skull can withstand," Juan said as Kitty fumbled with the doorknob to leave.

He stood in the doorway and watched as she went running out to her car, sobbing loudly the whole time, and roared away, tires screeching, down the quiet street, out into the flat darkness. After her tail-lights disappeared his whole body slumped and he groaned, almost inaudibly, and raked at his face with his fingers.

After a while he turned around and looked at me for a second, his eyes vacant and moist. He went to sit on the couch, changed his mind, stood at the window and stared out. He began nodding his head, like someone trying to muster conviction.

"Rita?" he called out, like I was far away, not just five feet from him. He knelt down in front of me and took the hat off his head, put it over his heart. I realized I was still holding the bat.

"Rita," he said, "marry me?"

For a moment I was simply dumbstruck, and then a terrific rush of joy and relief began building up inside me, a feeling I gave into completely until I looked into Juan's eyes. What I saw there was not love or the need to be loved or anything like it—it was the same look he had waiting for Kitty to club him on the head, the same look he'd worn most of the last six months. The hope of a long happy life together was the furthest thing from his mind. I knew exactly what he was thinking, kneeling there in front of me. He was thinking of being dragged down by an impossible weight, clawing for air, lungs filling with black water until they burst.

I dropped the bat and walked out of the room, left Juan

kneeling by the window. There was nothing else to do; I felt like I'd fallen down a flight of stairs.

All that night I cleaned. I had let the house go to pot over the last six months and suddenly I wanted it clean again. I started with the bathroom and worked my way through the house: swabbing floors, scrubbing walls, vacuuming, washing clothes, dusting the light fixtures and underneath the beds. Juan would occasionally look in on me, but he didn't say a word. By midnight I had the house spotless and I didn't even take a break before starting in on the cooking. I made a huge vat of soup, casseroles, rice and beans, stir fry, whatever I could find in the house. I cooked all night and put the food in Tupperware containers and stuffed them into the refrigerator until it could hold no more.

By dawn I had a small overnight bag packed with a few of my things. I called everyone I could think of, all of our mutual friends, and explained the situation and asked them to help keep an eye on Juan. I even called the county mental health division and made them promise to send someone over as soon as they could manage it.

Once I was sure I had done everything there was to do, I went and found Juan in the front room, sitting on the floor with Louise in his lap. He might have been crazy, but he knew exactly what was happening—he grabbed me, pushed his face into my chest and held on tight. I hugged him and told him once more, for the thousandth time, that I loved him. I told him to feed Louise and give her the medicine she needed every two weeks. Juan didn't say anything at all, just kept his face buried in my neck and finally he let go of me.

The sun wasn't quite over the trees when I got into my car and pulled out of the driveway with no clear idea of where I might be headed. I drove slowly down the street, in the direction of the freeway entrance. As I got further from town, out into the sagebrush and piñon pine, even with my heart breaking I felt a sense of freedom I'd never felt before, like a great heaviness falling away, and it was as if I was rising above the road, into the white morning sky, floating.

Junk Court

I'm Bach Abercorn, maintenance man at the Cinnamon Ridge Apartments here in Holbrook, Arizona. You break it I fix it, as they say. That's why I'm late. I was down in my basement shop putting on my Pumas when Ginny the secretary from upstairs called and said someone's disposal was jammed. I told her I was already late for my game but she kept on saying, emergency, emergency, using the word like a knife to threaten me. So I went up to 12-D and pulled out a Donald Duck baby spoon that was twisted up in the disposal's blades. This is what I do.

Now I've got my head out the window of my GMC, letting the wind blow my ears back. It is one of those queer summer days in the middle of February and for the first time in ages I've got the weight of a woman on my mind. I'm on my way out of Holbrook and into the open spaces of scraggly cedars and piñon pine. Holbrook sits out on the high desert plateaus of northeastern Arizona and is the proud home of petrified wood and dinosaur bones. In movie towns they have wooden Indians in front of their drugstores. We have stoned Indians in front of ours.

I have to pick up Morris for our Friday hoopfest at the Junk Court. It's called the Junk Court not only because it is right in the middle of old Redrock Junkyard, but also because of the brand of garbage ball that is played there. No one seems to know why the man who used to own the place built a basketball court in the middle of all the junk. He must have been a real old-fashioned basketball lover. I like to imagine the old guy, whoever he was, silhouetted against the tangled metal, shooting two-handed jumpers in the twilight.

Morris has a little house out here on the Old Dump road. He sold his Land Cruiser to buy it. Morris says if you don't have a house, you have nowhere to hang your heart. He's out on the front lawn, lying on his stomach and reading a book when I come roaring in on a storm of gravel. He's wearing sunglasses and a bandanna around his head to keep his hair out of his eyes. Morris gives me a huge smile that makes me wince. He's got a front-tooth gap you can fit four stacked quarters into. When we go out together I remind him to keep the grinning to a minimum.

Back on the road, Morris says, "You haven't convinced me."

Morris and I argue. That is what our friendship is based on—the conflict of minds. Our current subject is abortion. Morris is trained in debate and uses technique on me. All I have to fall back on is common horse sense. We talk about everything: women, politics, God, the capital gains tax. We make it a point not to agree.

Right now I can't think about abortion, can't formulate any theories. I've got sunshine on my nose and the thought of this girl that feels like a wandering tumor in my skull. I saw her yesterday during lunch break at the Rhino's Horn Inn. She must be a student at the little college in town, Northland Pioneer. She was sitting in the booth across from me, doing her best to eat. She had some kind of disease or condition that made most of her body jerk and twitch. It took her three or four tries before she could get half a forkful of corn in her mouth, her arm and head jerking around like that. I watched her and my throat thickened up and I could hardly breathe. What was it I felt right then? Sadness? Respect? Guilt? Love? Maybe I felt all of them at once, I still can't say. I got up to give her a hand or say something nice, but instead I turned away and walked right out the door, hurting.

All this has been banging around in my head since then. For me to think about one girl for more than fifteen minutes is an amazing thing.

"I don't know," I say and assume a thoughtful look so maybe Morris will understand my state of seriousness.

"About what?" Morris says.

I want to explain the whole thing to Morris, tell him what I'm feeling. I have to talk to someone and if I can talk to any-one, it's Morris. But what do I say to him? Hey, Morris, I saw this girl who has a handicap or a disease or something and I think maybe I love her?

It just doesn't work that way.

When we get to the Junk Court everybody is shooting around waiting for us. I'll be dammed if I don't get nervous like I used to when I stood in the dark locker room, needing to pee something fierce and waiting to take the floor for the varsity

Holbrook Redskins. We have Indian reservations all around us, Hopi to the northwest, Apache to the south, Navajo to the east. We're the only non-Indian team in the region and we're called the Redskins. Morris says the irony is tremendous.

"Thank you for coming," my cousin Pacer says. Pacer has blond hair down to his ass and a bad attitude that goes farther than that. When there is a fight he is generally in the middle of it.

The sun is hot and it feels good to strip off my shirt. Me, Pacer, Chief and John Boy are always skins. We've kept the same teams from the very beginning. We match up almost perfect. Right now it is ninety-four games to ninety-one in favor of the shirts. We keep a tally scratched into the hood of an old green Studebaker. A few times the snow or ice storms have stopped us, but we've always played right through rain or high winds. One time we played in a pea-soup fog. We were taking shots without being able to see the basket; you just had to get a feel for where the hoop was.

Juice is down at the other end, hitting set shots from out in the washing machine parts. He has the gift of softness; his shots never seem to rattle the rim. The ball comes down wet, he shoots it so high. He is far and away the most talented of us, but he's lazy, doesn't play stiff defense, comes to the games sometimes with a Seagram's Seven buzz. Juice is haunted by potential. He stole my old girlfriend, got her pregnant, married and divorced her, all in less than a year. Whenever I see him I tell how grateful I am it was him instead of me.

Chief shoots the do-or-die. We don't let Juice shoot it anymore because the man just doesn't miss unless somebody's got a hand in his face. Chief puts it up, it comes down hard off the back of the iron and Chief dies. Shirts get the ball first. Jimmy Hammond flies low right over us in his little crop duster and we all pause to give him the bird.

I guard Rabbi, my older brother. Me and Rabbi guarding each other doesn't do much for our brotherly relationship. We only live a couple of miles away from each other but here at basketball games is the only time I see him. We're not Cain and Abel, but things could be better.

Shirts bring the ball up. Mugsy is at the point, smiling and yo-yoing the ball by his hip.

"What are you grinning at, prick?" says Chief, who is guarding Mugsy.

"You mothers are smoke," Mugsy says, his big, bald face shining.

Mugsy tries to drive the lane but Chief picks him clean and takes the ball down to the other end for an easy lay-up. "Stay out of my kitchen," Chief roars, "I'm gonna clean up!" Even though Chief is an Indian and should be soft-spoken like the rest of them, he talks more trash than any of us. He is a pleasure to have around, if he's on your team.

Francisco is the only one who doesn't make a lot of noise around here. Francisco is an ex-wetback from Guadalajara who, a few months back, was instantly transformed into a proud American citizen. To him, this simply means that he won't have to steer clear of the border patrol anymore. Francisco is the only one of us without a nickname. With a name like Francisco who needs one, I say. I am writing a paper about nicknames for my Evolution of the English Language class at Northland Pioneer, where I study off and on. It's not like we have a drought of nicknames around here. You have to work hard at *not* having one.

We all start out jittery, missing our shots and throwing the ball away, but pretty soon we settle in and it's almost like we're doing a dance we've been practicing for years. Rabbi is really hitting them from outside today and I have to play right in his shorts until he misses a few. When he's got the ball I keep one

hand on his back and the other poking at the ball. He swats
my hand away and pushes me back.

We take a break with the game tied at fifty. Chief is really
lighting it up for us, doing the Apache run-and-gun to per-
fection. He is playing like his idol, Isiah Thomas, spinning
and whirling and taking running scoop shots that kiss off the
backboard and drop through the bucket with a sweet snap of
the net.

We all have our idols. Mine is Larry Bird. I would kiss the
man's sweaty toes if he would let me. Every time I watch him
play it makes me emotional. I shoot the same way he does—
flat-footed with the ball cocked by the side of his head. I play
hard-nosed, straight-up ball. I used to comb my hair the same
way he does. I don't dunk.

We lie down in the middle of the court. Sweat rolls off us
and makes little puddles in the cement. We pass around the
water and Gatorade and look into the sun. Juice sits on a rusty
swamp cooler and chugs an Old Milwaukee. Francisco hums
Julio Iglesias with feeling.

"How's your vacation going?" Morris says to Pacer. They
work together at the power plant and do their best to act like
they enjoy each other's company.

"Been painting my house," Pacer says, tucking a strand of
hair behind his ear. "Get this. Yesterday I was taking the
storm gutter down and Edna Longley, the little divorced girl
who moved in across the street, was out with her platoon of
obnoxious kids in front of her house."

Pacer goes into this long explanation about how the
woman fell to pieces on her front lawn, shrieking and sobbing
and tearing the grass up. Turns out Pacer offered to take her
kids for awhile and ended up loading them in the back of his
truck and hauling them over to the bowling alley to play video
games. He takes his time, giving us every detail.

"The rug rats cost me forty-seven quarters," Pacer says. "I bought the baby one of them big Tootsie Rolls and it never made a peep."

"You took her childs?" Francisco says with that little accent the women love.

"Damn straight," Pacer says, looking rather proud. "A woman breaking down like that, somebody had to do something."

"Shit," John Boy says.

We all contemplate the story Pacer has told us. Nobody knows what to say. Usually we fill the air with talk about sex or sports, something with a joke or a lie in it, nothing serious like this. I wonder if now would be the right time to say something about the girl I saw, but before I can say anything John Boy pipes up about a show he saw on TV last night where a father killed all his children with a propane torch. He finishes with a solemn, "True fucking story."

All at once we get up and decide not to endure any more stories.

We shoot around a bit to find our distance before we get busy again. We huddle and decide our strategy will be to let Chief shoot a lot. This is exactly what happens and Chief carries us home, does us proud.

When the game is done it's getting dark and we gather up our things, talking about certain points of the game, letting sweet exhaustion settle into our bones. We get into our trucks and drive away from each other. Skins have won number ninety-two and the momentum is swinging our way like something out of the dark; we are closing the gap.

Some days I wake up chock-full of impossible questions. This morning, with hot air balloons in the cold sky over the desert, they are not the universal questions I am normally inclined

towards. Today they are questions about who I am. Am I the
fix-it man who plays basketball and drives a cowboy truck or
am I the guy who writes papers at the college and likes poetry written by women who kill themselves? Why can't I mas-
ter the cross-over dribble or simple iambic pentameter? Who
am I to love a diseased woman I've never met?

I'm fixing coffee and Hannah is burning off a hangover in
my bed. Hannah is someone I know from my language class.
We've done study sessions. Last night she went to a party here
in the complex and showed up at my door around midnight,
doing the Budweiser two-step and asking me if I knew where
her car was. I decided letting her stay would be better than
scouring hell's half-acre for her car. She slept on one side of
my bed and made high whistling noises through her nose. It
reminded me of when Trooper, my black-and-tan hound,
used to sleep in bed with me and make the same kind of racket. Even though it's been three years since Trooper died, it's a
sound that still comforts me.

Hannah wakes up slowly and takes coffee without saying
anything. Her face looks like it needs to be ironed, but I've
seen worse. I wonder if her brain has kicked in.

"You were sauced last night, so I took the liberty of remov-
ing your shoes, that's all," I say.

"I remember, I remember," she says. One of her ears is
missing its golden hoop.

"How's your term paper coming?" I say. The blank look she
gives me tells me that I should stop asking questions until
she gets everything together. She goes into the bathroom and
puts her head under the bathtub faucet. "This will cure me," she
says over the roar of water. She comes out dripping and much
fresher. Her curly blond hair is now dark and plastered to her
head.

"I lost a boyfriend yesterday," she says.

"Not lost in the dead sense of the word, I hope," I say.

"No, just lost as in gone for good," she says.

I am not the sort of handyman that James Taylor sings about. I'm not handy with love and I don't fix broken hearts. Some women just don't understand this. The women in this complex, most of them college girls, see me with my tools, unclogging a sink or replacing a rusty P-trap and for some reason they think I'm capable of anything. When I'm in their apartments they tell me their problems, ask advice, invite me to dinner, to bed. I'll always listen and give advice when I can, but I don't accept many invitations. It's not the way I was raised.

"I can't help you," I tell Hannah.

I have a heart of my own to deal with.

The girl's name is Victoria. She lives in a condo and has a nervous system disorder with a complicated name. All this I found out from Hannah, who works in the records office. Hannah seems to be always underfoot these days. I guess she has to have a man in her life at all times and right now, I am it. I've explained my feelings to her so she won't have any expectations. When you get right down to it, it's kind of nice this way.

Victoria is a sophomore in botany. I've been reading about plants and flowers and I'm looking into buying a fern. Whenever I do any thinking these days it's about my paper or Victoria, who I've seen again, this time at the library. She was paging through a book as thick as a birthday cake. I watched her through rows of Jonson and Donne like some kind of peeping Tom. I couldn't see her face, just her long, blue-black hair. Her hand was jerking so bad she ripped some of the pages when she turned them.

Hannah has gone to the supermarket to buy tortillas for

chimichangas, which are my favorite. I'm not sure why she does all this for me. Morris says he would put his five dollars on her deep-seated desire to nurture. She makes my bed when she comes over. She washes my socks.

I'm waiting on Rabbi, who is coming over for lunch. I've figured it up and this will be only the fourth time he has ever come to visit. He drives up in his jacked-up Dodge. One of the more difficult questions I've been asking myself lately: why do we all have trucks if the only thing we use them for is to throw empty beer cans in the back?

Rabbi does not work at the moment but would join the circus before asking any help from me. He lets himself in and hangs his hat on the antelope antler above the door.

"Where's the girl?" he says. Rabbi is one of those big men who never feels the need to say anything nice. We have the same straight hair and long chin and our noses are similar, except his is a larger version which has been broken a time or two.

I say, "She went out for food. Chimichangas."

Rabbi nods and pages through an old issue of *Outdoor Life*. I get up and grate some cheese and he says, "I'm looking into gold mining. I have a friend who made twenty thousand in only two months up to the Yukon."

"Think you might go?" I say.

Rabbi shrugs. "We'll have to see. So what's with this girl? Living together, even. Never thought you had it in you."

"Hannah doesn't live here. She's just around a lot. There's nothing going on."

Rabbi tilts his head back and scratches his neck, looking down the bumpy length of his nose at me.

Hannah comes busting through the door with sacks of groceries and a messed-up hair-do. She says, "Lines."

I introduce them and Rabbi gives Hannah a look-over like

he's making an appraisal on a car. Hannah nods at him and takes the cheese from me and begins to grate. Outside, a long line of honking cars passes, with people hanging out the windows, whooping and yelling. The aftermath of a Mexican wedding.

"You would think somebody would have a pineapple, for God's sakes," Hannah says, grating with a vengeance. "I looked all over town so we could have fresh piña coladas. There wasn't so much as a coconut."

Rabbi looks at me. The way Hannah is acting you would think she is somebody's wife.

We sit down to eat and there is a general silence until Hannah says, "Rabbi's an interesting name. You don't do bar mitzvahs do you?"

Rabbi looks at her for a second, then says, "Never."

In my paper, I'm using Rabbi, whose real name is Lyle. I was there when Lyle's nickname was born. This was back when we were kids living in Oregon. We were the only ones home and I was inside watching cartoons and he was out climbing around on the oak trees behind the house. One particular tree had a good-sized laundry line hook screwed into one of its big lower branches. It seems that Rabbi forgot about that hook. He straddled the big branch and slid down it, butt-first. When he came up to the sliding glass door and tapped on it, his face was as gray as ashes and black streams of blood stained his jeans down to the knees. I opened the door for him and he said, "I think my tally-whacker's cut off." I called an emergency number from a bulletin board by the phone while he sat on the couch like a zombie and watched Woody Woodpecker. The medics came and took him away and left a note for my folks about where Rabbi was, where to call, etc. When my mother got home and saw blood all over the couch she wanted to know what happened. I told her that Rabbi had cut off his tally-whacker and two guys in orange shirts came in the house and carried him away. My dad used to say my mother was never quite the same after that.

Rabbi didn't lose his tally-whacker after all, but it took twenty stitches to keep him in possession of it. We like to say that he was the first Rabbi ever to perform his own circumcision.

I tell this story to everybody. Rabbi hates me for it.

When he is done eating, he wipes his mouth with the tablecloth, stands up, slaps his hat on his head, says, "We'll be seeing you. Stay sober if you get the chance."

When we're on the porch and out of Hannah's earshot, Rabbi gives me the old elbow nudge and says, "You're not getting any nookie?"

I don't know if it was the nickname incident or what, but Rabbi never has had any luck with women.

There is nothing sadder than a Camp Fire girl gone bad. This is what Hannah says to me one night after our language class. She has convinced me to sit on the campus lawn with her and look for meaning in the stars.

I say, "You were a Camp Fire girl?"

She says, "I was."

"Have you ever eaten a lizard?" I say.

She says, "No."

"I have," I say.

Hannah snorts like a farm animal. "At one of our meetings we made goals for our lives and put them in a time capsule. We dug a hole with those tiny gardening shovels and buried it out in front of the community center."

"For posterity," I say.

"No," she says. "For ourselves. Our leader, Mrs. Teal, dug

them up and sent them to each one of us. Mine said I was going to find the cure for a big disease and become the governor of Texas."

"There's still time," I say.

Hannah props her head against my shoulder and we take in the universe. It seems that Hannah has fallen for me. She has seen me fix furnaces and light fixtures. Her toothbrush is now a permanent part of my medicine cabinet.

I am coming to know myself as a coward. I can't tell Hannah to leave and I can't approach Victoria. I saw her today—for the first time in a week. She was in the computer lab typing, one quivering finger at a time. It took me an hour just to calm myself down.

I don't say anything about Victoria to Hannah, like I used to. I know it would make her like me all the more. Instead, I talk to myself about Victoria. I carry on the most private of conversations. I imagine what I would say to her, what questions I would ask. Maybe I would ask things like: Do you write poetry? Have you ever considered suicide?

The tag on my jockstrap reads, "The Duke." "The Duke" is the only thing I have on at the moment. I am jumping around on my bed with an invisible microphone in my hand and I'm singing "Helter Skelter" along with the Beatles. I pause to feel ridiculous now and then.

Hannah comes in without knocking and I bounce right off the bed and into the closet. I cover myself with a stray towel.

She comes in my room and turns the music down. She is a shiny wonder in spandex. I have never noticed her body until now. There is some definite firmness there.

"How about a run?" she says.

"I've got basketball today," I say, tucking the towel around my waist.

Her shoulders make a sudden drop and she lets out a sigh. "God, you're busy," she says.

I shrug as I tiptoe into the bathroom where my clothes are. I put on my shorts and tanktop while she picks up things off the floor.

"Can I go with you?" she says. "I'm going with you."

"No." I say. "You'll hate it."

"What, you don't allow women? What is this?"

"It's not that. No woman has ever wanted to go." This is a lie—on a few occasions a wife or a serious girlfriend has attended a game at the Junk Court. I've never been good at lying but I hope this one will stick.

"I'll be the first then," Hannah says. She finishes making my bed and goes out to wait for me in the truck. If I had any spine to speak of I would go out there right now and command her to stay home. But like I said before, I'm soft and a coward.

When we pick Morris up he gives me a look like I have just set his mother on fire. Hannah ignores Morris completely. Morris and Hannah hated each other from the first time they met. I'm still not sure why.

I am worried that Hannah's coming with me to the Junk Court will be interpreted in the wrong way. I give it a week before people start asking us when we plan to tie the knot. At least I can carry on my obsession with Victoria in private. I have written poems to her, poems that are filled with crusty language that rhymes. I've made up a song on my guitar about her that can be sung with a twang. Nobody knows it, but I'm a tortured man.

None of the boys pay too much attention to Hannah. My worst fear was that she was going to ask to play. But she just sits in the truck looking sour. Of course, I get all the dirty jokes and questions from everybody on the court. I'm glad Hannah has her windows rolled up.

We wait for Rabbi and Mugsy to show, but when Mugsy comes, he's got somebody else in the seat next to him. He announces that Rabbi is getting ready to leave for the Yukon in search of gold, so he brought a friend of his, Red Hall, to take Rabbi's spot.

Red is tall and skinny and has a shaved head that gives him the look of a Holocaust survivor. He has a tattoo on his arm that says in plain letters, *Generic Tattoo*. This is the man that is replacing my brother.

As we get into it, I feel my eyes get blurry and my body gets a little weak. My first four shots rip the net and I know that I'm riding a hot streak, an unnatural phenomenon that happens to me every once in a while. I am not Larry Bird anymore, but an incarnation of Dominique Wilkins, slashing down the lane, pumping and wheeling, dunking hard with two hands. The guys on my team just feed me the ball and watch. Red, who is guarding me, has something akin to fear in his eyes. It's not fair to humiliate him his first day out, but I can't make myself slow up. I feel empty and loud like a desert wind. Nothing can stop me from taking it to the hole.

The game ends and we have blown the Shirts out of the water. I lie down in the dirt by the court and watch a crow slip across the sky. I decide I better get up and interview Red about the history of his nickname. I have shin splints and one of my fingers is dislocated. There is a long, bleeding scratch on my forearm. The pain lets me know I'm alive.

Rabbi must be in Montana by now. After the basketball game I went home and found a note on my screen door. It was written on the back of a grocery receipt and said, *Borrowed your tent. Buy you a new one. See ya later, Lyle.*

Hannah is cutting my hair in the kitchen and Morris has arranged himself on the couch with a bowl of Corn Pops. It is early Friday night and I just got finished draining the water heater of an extensive Taiwanese family in A-16. The heater was making ticking noises and they were sure it was going to explode. While I drained the sediment out of it, they kept on making explosions with their hands and mouths and pointing to the water heater.

"Bach," Hannah says, "sit still." She says my name the way a chicken would.

Hannah is a graduate of beauty school and wants to do something with my hair. I tell her to keep her somethings to herself and just chop it off. She giggles and keeps on snipping. We've been at this for an hour now.

I forget to sit still and Hannah puts a notch in my ear with the scissors. Hannah shrieks and I lean forward saying, "Oh, crap, oh." Hannah grabs my head and sucks the blood from my ear like she's administering to a rattlesnake bite. When she's finished she smacks her lips.

Morris is watching *Jeopardy* and getting most of the questions wrong. He's mad because we don't argue much anymore. He doesn't like it that I practically have a woman living in my house who I don't even love. He thinks Rabbi is an asshole for not saying goodbye to me before heading to the Yukon. He says Rabbi never knew shit from Shinola.

Truth be known, I don't know the difference either, but I'll never admit it.

I have been forced into a Saturday night lie. Hannah wanted me to go with her tonight to see a Zuni fertility dance with her anthropology class. I told her I had already made plans with Chief and Morris to play poker, when in fact I'm going to meet Victoria and get this over with. Somehow I'm lying to a girl I have never kissed for a girl I don't even know.

It's a windy night and I have dust in my teeth. Victoria's

condo is next to a squatty little Catholic church that looks as if
it was slapped together with mud a few hundred years ago. A
cross stuck in the top is lit with Christmas lights. Most likely
it is the church where the Mexicans had their wedding the
other day.

Victoria lives on the second floor. I park my truck at the
curb and creep up the outside stairs like a burglar. My stomach feels like there's something dying in it. I stand in front of
her door without any idea of what to do, looking for clues in
the woodgrain. Today I woke up and decided that I can't be a
coward any longer, that this thing with Victoria is one of those
now or never kind of things.

I contemplate the door, feeling quite lousy at this point. It
takes me a minute to work up enough gumption to press the
doorbell. A chunky, over-made-up girl answers the door. She
is the kind of girl my father would have fondly called a
"heifer."

"Victoria here?" I say.

The girl retreats into the hallway and comes back saying,
"She says you can go back there, second door on the left."

I cough out a thanks and head back into the dark hallway,
feeling like I'm making the descent into hell. Victoria's door
is open and she's sitting on her bed, staring at the opposite
wall. There are plants hanging from the ceiling. A large
sketch of a nude woman is tacked to the wall over her head
and there are other drawings around it.

She says, "Hello," and I stare at the sketch of the nude.

"You can sit down if you want," she says. Her skin is bone-
white and dotted with the tiniest freckles. Her hair reflects
the light of the lamp and her voice is huskier than I imagined.
The rest of her is covered with an afghan. She looks very
sleepy. She stares at me for a long time.

"Nice to meet you," I say. "I just came over to talk."

She gives me another long, droopy-eyed stare. She says, "I've just taken my medication. It slows me down some."

I notice that her body isn't jerking or twitching. I sit on the cedar chest across from her bed. During the day I concocted all kinds of excuses for being here, but I can't think of any of them right now.

"Are these your drawings?" I say.

She says, "Bingo."

I nod.

"I've never seen you before," she says.

"No," I say. "I just stopped by to visit."

This seems to be enough of an explanation for her. She puts her head back and stretches her arms. She says, "I'm thirsty. Could you get me some water?"

I go out to the kitchen. The heifer is planted on a bean bag watching a real-life show about sex scandals and murders.

"Victoria needs a glass of water," I say.

"Cupboard over the sink," she says without looking my way.

When I get back to Victoria I find her doubled over with her face in her lap. She looks up at me and says, "I could be better."

She takes the water in great gulps, streams of it running out the sides of her mouth. I put my hand on her back and take the glass from her. She leans into me and says, almost with a drawl, "Let's have the lights off."

I turn off the lights and go back to her. She pulls the blanket around me and puts an arm around my neck. She says into my ear, "I don't know who you are." We lie there in the dark until she struggles off the bed and crawls into the bathroom across the hall. I stand over her as she vomits into the toilet. In the bright light of the bathroom there are little whales on the walls, spouting water into the air. I clean her up and help her back to bed. She shudders and puts her hands between her knees. Cars hum by below the window. I listen as her breathing slows down and levels off.

A couple of times in the night I wake up and she is making a high wailing sound. It is a sound that makes me afraid. I think about putting a pillow over her face or holding her so tight that she can't make the noise anymore, but she stops and stays quiet. I wake up again at six-thirty and stand up, rubbing the grit out of my eyes. I feel like I've been sleeping on a pile of rocks. Victoria is curled up in her blanket, her hair spread around her, quiet as a handkerchief.

I go out into the kitchen and the girl from last night is there, making coffee. She is wearing some kind of fast-food uniform.

She says, "Have you been here all night?"

The girl offers coffee and I take it. She sizes me up over the rim of her mug.

"She threw up last night," I say.

"The medicine she has to take to help her sleep makes her sick. She throws up every night."

"She can't get other medicine?" I say.

The girl shakes her head. "It's all there is."

The coffee burns my tongue. I get up and give my legs a good stretch. As I go out the door the girl says, "She has a boyfriend. He's legally blind."

I sit in my truck with my hands on the steering wheel. I can't find my keys. It is still dark but the sun is waiting just below the blue mesas. It is chilly and the air smells like wood smoke.

I think about Rabbi up north of the border. I imagine him in overalls and a big hat, holding up a pan of dirt speckled with gold. He has a rough beard and he cooks pork and beans over a campfire and eats it out of the can. I wonder if he misses the basketball.

I look through my glove compartment, thinking there might be a spare key in there. All I find are lottery tickets, gum wrappers and a map of Mexico that smells like beer. I sit back and take account of everything I know. I know there are things waiting to be fixed. I know that Victoria will never know my name and that there will be a game at the Junk Court next week, same place, same time. As for things I know for sure, this is as far as it goes.

The rest I can't be sure of. Maybe I'll find my keys. Maybe I'll go home and Hannah will be there in the kitchen with white sunlight in her face, fixing hash browns and sausage and wondering where I've been. Maybe I'll tell her to leave, or ask her to stay for good, I just can't say. Maybe I'll tell her to pack up her things because we're going to the Yukon to get my tent back.

Letting Loose
the Hounds

———————————————●———————————————

Goody Yates was a mess. He shambled along the side of the road, slump-shouldered and bleeding from the mouth, his head stuffed with cotton, pain and delirium duking it out in the pit of his mind. He didn't know where he was or what he was doing, barely knew *who* he was, but the one thing he did know was this: if he didn't get some relief soon, if the pain in his head continued to attack him like the firebreathing beast it was, he was going to throw himself under the wheels of a passing car, just go right ahead and end the whole damn thing.

There had been something keeping the agony in check, something that had numbed everything, settled over his brain like heavy mist, white and soothing, but now it seemed to be wearing off. Goody whimpered like a baby and swallowed a mouthful of blood.

A primer-gray El Camino pulled over next to him, spraying gravel. "Why are you standing in a ditch?" somebody inside the car wanted to know.

Goody hadn't realized that he was in a ditch, but he looked down and sure enough, there he was in a weed-clogged ditch. He wished to God there was some water in the ditch. He was hotter than hell.

"You okay?" the person in the El Camino said. "Did somebody lay you upside? Your face looks like a pumpkin."

Goody tried to tell the guy to fuck off but he couldn't seem to talk. He made a try at opening his mouth which set the nerves in his jaw smoldering like lit fuses.

"Stand up out of that ditch and get in the car," the man said. "I'll give you a lift. You appear to me like a person who needs help."

Goody had to agree. He needed a lot of help. He was in bad shape all the way around. He got in the car and was able to get a view of this guy for the first time. He looked like a squat, grizzled version of General Custer: the handle-bar mustache, the longish golden-blond hair waving out from under a stained Peterbilt baseball cap. Cool green hungover eyes.

They started back onto the road, the El Camino belching and shuddering like a sick old man. Empty beer cans and rifle shells rolled around on the floor.

"Where to?" Custer said, his voice full of cigarettes. "Hospitals are good in situations like this."

Goody shook his head, which was a mistake; fireworks went off in front of his eyes. He didn't want to go to a hospital. If he knew anything at all, it was that hospitals cost money and one thing he did not have in this world was money.

He leaned back and put his head against the top of the seat

and watched the pine trees zipping past. The steady *lug-lug-lug* of the car's engine soothed him. He heard Custer talking but couldn't make out the words. He felt like he was falling down a very deep hole and before he had time enough to be grateful, he'd passed into sleep.

When Goody woke he found himself in a whole new universe of pain. The haze in his head had cleared up considerably, which was not a good thing; everything was as clear and excruciating as it could be. He was so hot it felt like his clothes were rotting off him. Custer helped him out of the car and the only thing Goody could think was: *I want to die, I really would prefer to die*. Custer stood him up, waited for him to get his balance and led him onto the porch of a small house, a cabin really, all by itself in the middle of a saltgrass meadow, set up on blocks off the muddy ground and surrounded by ponderosa pines. Next to the house was an orange Le Mans sedan and a large, chain-link kennel where a bunch of hounds—fifteen or twenty—stretched out in the afternoon sun.

Custer rattled the handle on the screen door, which was stuck, and finally, unable to get it to work, yanked the entire door off its hinges and sailed it over the porch railing and into the mud. Inside there were various broken objects scattered around: a splintered chair, a coffee table which appeared to have been sawn in half, an old-time jukebox with its electronic guts spilling out. In one corner of the living room were stacked a bunch of wooden milk crates filled with odds and ends. After helping Goody onto a small couch missing its cushions—the only intact piece of furniture in the room— Custer handed him a pink slip of paper and said, "You dropped this in the car when you fell asleep."

The paper was crumpled and stained and at the top was

printed: *H. Felix Manderberry, D.D.S., 149 South Mountain Road, Alpine, Arizona. (602) 337-2093.* Underneath, in the kind of indecipherable longhand doctors and dentists are known for, was a prescription for something, Goody couldn't tell what. As soon as he saw the prescription he remembered, as if recalling a dream: earlier today, possibly only an hour or so ago, this dentist, this H. Felix Manderberry, had fed sodium pentobarbital into his veins and removed four impacted wisdom teeth from Goody's mouth. He remembered waking up in the chair and some nurse looming above him in the harsh light, asking: *Are you awake Mr. Yates, can you open your eyes?* She handed him the prescription and went on, giving her prepared speech on what foods he could eat, when to take the medication, and so forth. Goody hardly got any of it; it was like he heard everything, but the moment the words entered his brain they just fell away. She left him, telling him to stay put for awhile until he felt fully himself, but Goody got right up and off he went, still caught in a fuzzy sleepworld, floating past the reception desk and the jittery, hand-wringing folks in the waiting room, opening the door to the outside, the mountain sun slapping him hard in the face. The next thing was getting into the El Camino and now here he was, in a remote cabin with Custer.

"First I thought you were a handicapped person that somebody had knocked around. I almost did something stupid like call the police, but then I saw this paper. Did they yank out all your teeth? Seriously, friend, you should see this, you've got a dirty dinner plate for a face."

Custer stomped around, looking for something, then went back into the bathroom. Goody heard a loud, wrenching groan and Custer came out with a mirror-medicine chest, plaster dust still falling from the screws that had secured it to the wall. He held the mirror in front of Goody.

"Take a look," Custer said. "They must have done some butcher work on you."

Goody's face was an unrecognizable lump of puffed-up flesh. Purple bruises had begun to show under his eyes and his face was so swollen his jaws were clamped shut. He had never seen anything so pathetic and obscene.

Custer said, "You didn't pick up your prescription, did you? I can tell you're ailing. Tooth pain is the worst there is."

Goody tried to form words without moving his jaw, but his tongue was as thick and dry as a balled-up tube sock and there was blood-clotted gauze still packed into the craters where his teeth used to be. "Uhhggl Gaawwd," was the best he could do. Finally, using half-assed hand gestures, he asked for something to write with. Custer searched and searched but the only writing utensil he could come up with was a fat blue marker. There wasn't a sheet of paper in sight.

"Just go ahead and write on the wall," Custer said, lighting up a cigarette. "I'm going to burn this place down soon enough anyway. Can't even stand the sight of it anymore."

With only a slight hesitation, Goody turned and wrote on the wall above the couch, *wisdom teeth   no drugs   you got anything?*

Custer squatted, opened the medicine cabinet, which was now on the floor, and surveyed its contents. A dusty shaft of sunlight coming through one of the windows fell on his blond hair, making it shine with a kind of soft, angelic glow. "She took most of her pills with her when she left. Oh, she loved her pills, by God." He began picking up small brown bottles, squinting to read their labels. "Something for toenail fungus, stool softener, Demerol, Dexedrine something-or-other—shit, I don't know what this stuff is. I've never swallowed a pill in my life. Hold on a second." He went into the kitchen and came back with a bottle of Wild Turkey, took a swig before handing it to Goody. "See if you can get some of this into you and I'll give this dentist a call so we can find out what in hell to do." He took the prescription and went back in the kitchen where the phone was.

Goody unscrewed the cap on the bottle, tilted back his head and did his best to pour some whiskey through his teeth, but there was still the problem of the clumps of gauze. *Fuck it,* he thought and gagged the gauze down. Misery had pushed him into a state of complete disregard.

One thing was certain: if he ever saw this Manderberry character again he'd reciprocate some of this pain. He'd known people who'd had their wisdom teeth out and were running around chewing on pretzels and candy apples the next day. Sure, sometimes there was some swelling, a little discomfort, but, good Lord, how could it be this bad?

Manderberry was a friend of his father—just the thought of it all, the whole twisted junk heap of his life, made him want to puke. Goody was twenty-eight years old, slashed, burned and abandoned by his girlfriend of seven years, up to his eyebrows in debt, and going into the Army in two weeks' time. Once there was no longer any doubt in his mind that his life was an irretrievable failure, he'd considered suicide but decided on the Army instead.

It was his father, a World War II vet with a wide and varied collection of medals, ribbons and patriotic lies, who convinced him to sign up. His father had told him that the Army dentists were assembly-line hack artists and if he needed any dental work done he should do it before he joined. Manderberry owed a favor to his father, who arranged the surgery at no cost to his son. In the carefree, oblivious years following high school, Goody's parents had supported him almost completely, but six years ago pulled the plug on him, telling him it was time to make his own way. His father had even helped him take out a loan to start his own landscaping business, but the whole thing went belly up. He tried again, this time with a pawn shop and with the same result: out of business in less than a year. Now he was the janitor at Speaking Pines Country Club, earning two dollars over minimum wage and cleaning up after puckered old men (including his father) who, when they pissed, had great difficulty reaching the urinal. He lived in the basement of a hardware store and his meal of choice was rice with ketchup on top. He was drunk much of the time, always lonely (all his high school friends gone away, moved on) and his most common fantasy consisted of punching out just about everyone he knew.

Nights, when he wasn't haunting the bars, he sat at his rickety table in the posture of some sullen, self-taught philosopher, writing long fuming letters to his ex-girlfriend, Dottie, who, just over a year ago, had become pregnant by him, aborted the baby without letting him know, and had run off to Phoenix, taking his torn and bleeding heart with her.

This is what was left of his life: He would give his four years to Uncle Sam, make enough money on the GI Bill to pay for college, and maybe by the time he was forty he'd be able to get a good job so he could start paying off all his debts. It seemed entirely fitting that such a sad and ridiculous fuck-up as himself could go in for a simple dental procedure and end up like this.

He heard Custer tell Manderberry's secretary that he didn't give a good goddamn that the dentist was on his way out at this moment. He needed to speak with him right away. It was a bona fide emergency.

"Mr. Dentist?" Goody heard him say. "Well, my friend here"—he dragged the phone and its cord out into the living room and Goody wrote *Goody Yates* on the wall—"Goody, he's been given the dirty deal. Apparently you did a hatchet job on his wisdom teeth and then let him wander out into the street still loopy on the gas. I picked him up on fifth north, didn't know where he was, bleeding out of the mouth. Now his face is so swole up he can't open his mouth and he's suffering like a goddamn Christian. I guess you didn't give him any painkillers, either."

Just then there was a long howl and the scratch-and-snarl sound of dogs fighting. It sounded like only two or three dogs to begin with, then escalated into a kennel-wide brawl: growling and yelping and clicking teeth. Goody could hear Custer trying to talk over the racket for a good thirty seconds before slamming down the phone, sticking his head out the window—the stench of dog shit coming through—and bellowing, "Hah, hah, hah, hah, HAH!"

Instant silence. One of the dogs ventured a weak whine, but that was it. Custer, red-faced and fierce, went back to the phone but nobody was on the line. "I told him to wait a second but the chickenshit must have run off. I was truly prepared to lay into that sucker. Seems like I can't do anything without having some kind of commotion from them," Custer said, pointing to the window. "I've been off the mountain eight days now and they're going stir-crazy. I've got a black-and-tan bitch out there, Lucy, she's the one causing all the calamity. She has to be out on a trail every few days or she gets bored and starts bullyragging the boys."

Goody kept tipping up the whiskey, getting it all over his face, letting it run down his neck. He was practically showering in it. He was feeling a little better now. The pain was there, red-hot as ever, but he didn't seem to notice it as much. He offered the bottle to Custer who took another stiff swallow.

"You and me, Goody," Custer said, wiping his mouth. "Been a good three months since I had someone to swap the shit with. Even if you have to write your comments on the wall like a graffiti artist." He pulled a milk crate from the corner, emptied out its contents on the floor—a blow dryer, a box of Kleenex, dozens of bottles of nail polish—and sat down in front of Goody. "I should tell you, before your dentist buddy got away I told him what drugs we had in the house and he said Demerol, two tablets every four hours, should get you through until you can make it to the pharmacy. He said it's your fault for walking out still under the gas. He said he won't accept responsibility for anything because he has the best lawyer in the county."

Goody wrote, *I'll piss in his gas tank.*

"There you go. Yes. Subversive activity, they call it. That's the way you have to conduct these things." He found the bottle of Demerol and opened it for Goody. It took all the whiskey-fortitude Goody had to fight back the ache in his jaw, to open his mouth just wide enough to get the tiny BB-sized pills past his teeth. Once he had downed the pills he relaxed, quit tensing himself against the pain. Just the possibility of relief was enough for him.

Goody wrote on the wall, *God bless the pharmacy.*

Custer took a long drag on his cigarette like he was gaining vital nutrients from it. Even though the dogs had quieted down, Goody could still hear them, just outside the window, breathing and shifting, a single lurking presence.

After a while Goody wrote, *Why so many dogs?*

"I hunt lions," Custer said.

Goody raised his eyebrows and Custer explained that he hunted and killed mountain lions for a living, that he had a permanent camp up in the Blue Wilderness Area where he stayed seven months out of the year. Right now the place was crawling with lions, lions that were killing an inordinate number of livestock; the Arizona Fish and Game had done a lousy job of wildlife management over the past few years, issuing multiple deer permits and severely limiting the lion hunts. Now everything was out of whack; the lions, who didn't have much choice, admittedly, were taking livestock— even the shy black bears were coming out of the woods to drag calves away—and the ranchers were paying good money to have the predators killed.

Goody hadn't noticed until now, but it seemed that Custer spoke with a slight southern drawl. *You from Texas?* he wrote.

"Please, Lord, no," Custer said. "Louisiana. When we moved out here I had it in my head I was going to join the Forest Service, you know, driving around in a jeep with a goofy hat on, being kind to trees. And now look at me. Just last week my dogs got a big she-cat in a juniper tree and the branch broke out from under her. She killed four of my boys before the rest tore her to pieces. By the time I got there the only recognizable thing they'd left me to verify the kill with was a right foreleg. I just about didn't get my money on that one, but that rancher ended up paying me because he knows I've got the best trained dogs around, and he might need us again. These dogs, loud and obnoxious as they are, are the best pack in the southern Rockies. They'll go after any scent I set them to—bear, bobcat, lion—don't matter, and they'll kill it if they can. They know I don't like the killing part so much, so sometimes they take care of it for me."

Goody didn't know what to say to that, so he just sat there, rolling the marker between his palms.

"Yeah, shit," Custer said, standing up and walking in a tight circle, smoothing his mustache with both forefingers. The sun was dipping behind the trees and shadows were beginning to eat up the room.

They sat there for awhile, facing each other, and Goody wrote, *You live with somebody else here?*

Custer seemed to read the sentence over five or six times. At first his face was blank but then it fell into a broken, cheerless smile. "Used to," was all he said. He got up again and stared at a spot on the wall, the smile sticking to his face like something that did not belong there. Goody was immediately sorry he'd asked the question.

"I'm still trying to get a hold on this." He kicked the wall and tried to laugh but wasn't really able to pull it off. He looked ready to tear the house apart with his hands. "I come home off the mountain last Sunday, tired and dirty and ready for a little female attention and Mary is *gone*, along with most of her stuff. She is now, at this moment, shacked up with Wallace Greer, a big worthless layabout with the mind of a shrieking chihuahua. The year Mary and me moved here from Baton Rouge, before I started up on the mountain, we'd go bowling Friday nights and he was always there and I'd catch him looking at her. I noticed, but I didn't think twice. I'd been saying to myself: I'm gone a lot, we've had our problems, our shouting matches, but Mary is good and faithful, Mary would never do such a thing, Mary wouldn't let a creeping Jesus like him come and steal her away, Mary is my *wife*."

Custer went over to the stack of milk crates and picked up a blue flannel shirt that was draped over one of them, held it out in his bony fist. His green eyes were burning in his head. "This is his shirt. I come home off the mountain and this man's *shirt* is on my bed. Right now, up on the mountain, lions are coming out of the trees and taking calves, and I'm down here, drinking too much and trying to find the guts to do something about this."

Custer took an antique-looking glass kerosene lamp off the table and fiddled with it, trying to bring the wick up, his battered fingers trembling. It was almost full dark now.

"Damn, I'm sorry," Custer said. "I didn't bring you here to

air out my sorrows. I'm mouthing off like a lunatic. Why don't you tell me something about yourself? Only thing I know about you is your name is Goody and you have a shitty dentist."

Goody just stared up at him and Custer said, "Do you have a job or something?"

Cleaning toilets, Goody wrote.

Custer nodded. "Girlfriend?"

Left me high and dry.

"Hell," Custer sighed.

Goody wrote, *You said it.*

The fact of it was, Goody didn't know what to say to Custer. He had only questions of his own: Was it really this bad? Was the world chock-full with the frustrated and betrayed? Everybody he met these days—mostly in bars, it was true—seemed to be stricken with heartache and fracture and fallen hopes. Goody could tell him something like, *Hey, I can relate to what you're going through*, but that would be about as comforting as a glass of ice water in the face.

Goody thought about what he might say about his life, about his father, king of the country club, and his alcoholic mother and his insurance salesman brother and wife and her beautiful, fake breasts and capped teeth. He thought about Dottie and the little lost baby, fetus, whatever it was, that they had made together, and he began to write it all on the wall, tried to make it come out with some sense so Custer could understand, but what came out instead were phrases and names and words and tangled scribbles that had no meaning at all except to express the blackness inside him; now that the Demerol had taken care of the pain in his mouth he could focus without distraction on the pain in his soul. He knew, as he wrote, that it was a jumbled mess, but he couldn't stop himself, he had that same driven feeling that came over him when he wrote fifteen-page furious, ranting letters to Dottie late at night; he wrote about plagued lives and human failure and our hapless attempts at fulfillment and the slow burn of anger and bitterness. He wrote all over the damn wall, standing up from the couch, his arm moving with a jerking twitch. Phrases such as *the milk of hatred* and *so many awful pleasantries* showed themselves; words like *trash* and *mockery* and *outrage* popped up occasionally, but mostly it was just a dark impulsive scrabbling that continued, almost with a life of its own, until the marker ran out of ink.

Goody hadn't noticed that the shadows in the room had fused together and night had moved in. Custer took a Zippo from his pocket and lit the kerosene lamp, holding it up to the ink-covered wall like an archeologist getting his first look at ancient hieroglyphics in a cave.

"Damn," he said in a low voice, putting his hand on Goody's shoulder. "What the fucking hell."

Goody sat slumped on the couch feeling nothing at all. He could hear Custer outside, clomping up and down the porch steps, loading things into the trunk of the Le Mans. He came into the house, his skin slick with sweat, even though it had turned into a cool night. Goody could tell, even in the indefinite light, that an unnatural calm had come over Custer. "I believe I've come to a decision here," he said, his features a patchwork of shadows. "I hate to ask, with the condition you're in, but I could use a little assistance."

Goody nodded: of course, anything at all. This man had gone out of his way to help him and even though he'd known him for only a few hours, and not under the best of circumstances, he felt closer to Custer than he had to anyone in quite awhile.

Outside the crickets were going mad, an almost deafening

sound, and the air was piney and sweet. He followed Custer to the gate of the kennel and the dogs were gathered there, the whole clustered pack of them, yapping and wagging their entire bodies, saliva swinging from the loose folds of their mouths. There were eighteen of them in all—black and tans, blue ticks, treeing walkers, redbones, a couple of bloodhound mixes—and their coats were oiled and sleek and their molten eyes like dozens of tiny perfect moons.

Goody helped Custer clip leashes to each of the dogs' collars and Custer put nine of them into the back and front seats of the Le Mans, and nine into the bed of the El Camino. "When she left, she took the pickup," he explained, a little embarrassed. "Technically it's hers. Her daddy gave it to us before we left. Anyway, I'm going to need you to drive one of the cars. Just follow behind—we won't be going too far."

Even if Goody wanted to ask what was going on he couldn't have. He sat in the El Camino and watched Custer go into the house one last time. When he came out, he lingered in the doorway, looking into the house for a moment, then pitched the kerosene lamp into the middle of the living room. Goody could hear the sound of the lamp's glass breaking, followed by the *thwump* of the kerosene igniting, and through the porch window he could see a blaze leap up, a flash that lit up the whole house, quickly died down, but didn't go out.

By the time they were out on the highway after driving one or two miles on a muddy two-track, Goody looked back and couldn't see flames, but there was definitely a smoky yellow glow lighting up the sky just over the tops of the trees. They drove north on the highway, eight or nine miles, up through Quemado Pass, until Custer pulled over next to a shiny red Dodge pickup parked at the side of the road.

A cool breeze was coming down off the peaks, rustling the

grass in the meadow that stretched out until it reached a dense
line of ponderosas, a ragged black cutout against the galaxy-
filled sky. Other than the wind, the only sound in Goody's ears
was the fierce thump of his heart.

Custer gathered the dogs, knotted their leashes together
and handed them over to Goody. The dogs snapped and
pranced and yowled, their own tiny mob. "Stand there real
firm and they won't get away from you," Custer said. "They're
a little crazed tonight. I haven't fed them in three days."

Custer went around to the passenger side of the Le Mans,
reached through the window, and came back holding Wallace
Greer's shirt, a ratty old flannel shirt that now seemed terribly
significant in the blue mountain light. "I've been following
him around the past week," Custer said, his face grim and
alive. "He comes out here every night to pick the mushrooms
that grow along the river about a half mile down that little
valley. Kind of mushrooms make you see crazy things. He
makes a bit of money selling them to the high school kids and
keeps the rest for himself. This is the son of a bitch my wife
ran off with."

Goody and Custer stood there for a moment, staring at
each other, and something like agreement or acceptance
passed between them. It felt to Goody like his insides, his
brain, all of him, was vibrating like a tuning fork.

Custer squatted down and held the shirt in front of the
dogs' noses and said, in a low growling voice," Seek out, seek
out," over and over again, almost like a chant. At the sound
of the command the dogs went haywire, sniffing and biting
the shirt until one ripped it out of Custer's hand and all of
them dove in on it, slashing it to tatters. They were pulling so
hard the leather was biting into Goody's hands—it was all he
could do to hold on—but when Custer released them from
their leashes, one by one, something loosened and gave way

inside Goody and he stepped forward and shouted—a stran-
gled cry that barely made it past his tongue and clenched
teeth—urging the dogs on, feeling a strange, hot thrill run
through him as he watched their black shapes moving across
the meadow, howling like demons, charging through the
dark beautiful night and into the trees.

The Opposite of
Loneliness

──────────○──────────

hough she doesn't like to admit it, the fact that I live with
three crazy people is the reason Ansie won't stop by the
house to visit. She's a little uncomfortable with Tormey and
Iris, but Hugh makes her really edgy; he's the one that greet-
ed her at the front door a few months ago with his withered,
low-slung balls dangling out the fly of his boxer shorts. It was
the first and only time she ever dropped by. "How can you
sleep in the same house with them?" she asked me once. "For
all you know one of them could be a murderer or a sex maniac. One morning you could wake up with a fork in your eye
or somebody's hands in your shorts."

For a while after I first met her she referred to them as
"those crazy people," but now, at least, I have her calling them

by their names. She told me that when she was a little girl living in Denver, she had a whacked-out uncle who would occasionally escape from the mental hospital and show up at her
house in the middle of the night, usually buck naked except
for a pair of aviator's sunglasses, yelling obscenities and digging up the front lawn, searching for the remains of his pet
parrot, Percival, who he remembered burying there years
ago. She says ever since then she's had a certain fear of
lunatics.

I keep telling her that they aren't lunatics, that they aren't
really even crazy—just a little different from the rest of us.
Once when I was trying to convince her of this she stopped me
cold, waving her hands in front of my face, and said, "My
fears are my own and they're not negotiable." I didn't really
know what she meant but I haven't pushed the issue since.
I'm certain that if I can get her together with them long
enough she'll realize how paranoid she's being.

Ansie is my best friend and a woman. I am still trying to
come to grips with this. After my first marriage came to a
quick end six years ago, I've been a little wary of females. I've
gone on dates, had my share of relationships, but they never
worked, never moved anywhere beyond the misunderstand-
ings and pettiness that so frequently occur between two people who are trying to love each other. But it's different with
Ansie and me. A few nights a week we get together at The
Dive, drink beer and exaggerate our lives. Sometimes we
catch a movie or play gin rummy and watch TV in the sou-
venir shop she owns and lives in. There has never been anything like romance between us, that is the key. Romance and
real friendship cannot happen simultaneously—it has taken
thousands of years of civilization for us to understand this.
Ansie and I are buddies; I've never had a better friend. But
there's still this thing about her coming over to the house.

A couple of days ago I was at the grocery store, throwing things in my cart as if there was a war on. I had come up with this idea of having a feast in commemoration of no more snow; snow had covered everything for so long and now there was none. I'm a native of Phoenix, and though having snow around was a novelty at first, snow, like anything, gets old after awhile. The sun had come up that day and eaten away the remains of winter, chunk by chunk, until all that was left was spring. I danced around the store and pitched produce into my cart; I felt like running a marathon.

I was out in the parking lot loading bags into my Subaru when I saw Ansie across the street test-driving a bright green wheelbarrow in front of the hardware store. She was doing figure-eights and ninety-degree turns on the sidewalk. She picked up her little dog Gogo, a horrid-looking chihuahua-boxer mix, and put him in it. He slid around on its slick painted surface, too scared to yap, his oily eyeballs rolling in his head.

I trotted across the street and invited Ansie to dinner. I told her she could bring Gogo too as long as he didn't puke all over everything.

"He only vomits when he eats milk products," she said, swinging her long black hair at me defensively. "I told you not to let Iris feed him that cheddar soup."

Even though she is on the downside of thirty-nine (a year older than me) she has smooth, light brown skin that most women would murder for. The turquoise rings she wears on her fingers are the same color as her eyes.

"Okay," I said. "No cheese for Gogo. Butter and yogurt will be banned. No way you can refuse now."

"Is this dinner just you and me, or everybody?"

"Well, I thought we could celebrate the changing of seasons. Maybe act like pagans for a few hours. I'm thinking dig a hole in the backyard and roast something on a spit. I would have to say that a celebration, at the very least, requires five people. If you and Gogo come there'll be six of us. I bought enough grub to feed the House of Representatives."

"Tonight?" she said, checking the pockets of her jeans and denim jacket, looking up at the empty sky for inspiration. She needed an excuse, but wasn't having any luck coming up with one.

"If you don't want to come, just say so," I told her.

"You said it, I didn't."

This Ansie is a tough one. I went back across the street and yelled over passing traffic that if she decided she wanted to be sociable, she could still stop by and maybe we'd share the leftovers with her. On the way out of the parking lot as I passed the hardware store, she stood on some bags of fertilizer, a wide, pretty grin on her face, and flipped me the bird.

The house we live in, a big ornate structure that was built by a polygamist family a century ago, sits back off the road in a stand of old aspens, just outside the city limits of Payson. It used to be the summer home of Frank Berger Jr., citrus king-pin of Arizona, who donated it to the city before he died. It sat around for a few years until the city came up with a good use for it: to house Payson's "developmentally challenged"—one of those gracious terms for people who are healthy and fairly self-reliant, but don't have all the faculties to make do entirely on their own. The idea was to take these people out of the state homes, or out of situations in which they were burdens on their families, and put them in a setting where they could be productive and more independent. All they needed was someone to supervise.

I saw the ad in the *Payson Primer* last June when I was up here trying to sell Kotex and condom machines to the bars and convenience stores. If there is a job worse than a traveling tampon and condom dispenser salesman, I would like to know about it. I went for an interview (one of only four applicants, I learned later) and began outlining anything in my background I thought might be relevant to the job: my three years in the Peace Corps, my Eagle rank in the Boy Scouts, my sociology degree; but the woman stopped me and said that no professional qualifications were required, that other than a clean criminal record, all I needed was patience, responsibility and love. I told them I've had those things my whole life and was just waiting for a chance to put them to good use. So eight months ago I traded the heat and bad water in Phoenix for the cool, piney air of Payson.

Right now we're all in the kitchen, getting our feast ready. I have the whole downstairs to myself and the others have their own separate rooms upstairs. Iris is pressing cloves of garlic and I've got Hugh at work stuffing peppers. Tormey is over by the stove watching the water boil. I consider myself lucky that there are only three of them for the time being. The city council is actively recruiting other candidates; they want to be able to claim that the house and the small budget that goes with it are being put to good use.

"Never, ever again," Tormey says to the water. He's dressed in his dark blue suit and quilted pink booties. He's seventy-four and his features are smoothed and blunted, worn down by the friction of passing years.

When I first started out, the state-appointed mental health specialist who drops by every other month or so advised me that, among other things, I should provide my charges with as much physical contact as possible. Though I didn't feel entirely comfortable doing it, I tried giving everybody hugs for the first few days. I've long since quit doing that, but Tormey picked up on it and now gives me a hug every time he sees me.

I'll leave the room to use the john and when I come back I get the kind of sincere embrace normally reserved for someone who has just returned from battle. Although, like Tormey, her mind and memory have been splintered by senility, Iris hasn't lost her savvy when it comes to cooking. She has a part-time job cooking for the inmates at the county jail. It's a sure thing those prisoners have never eaten better in their lives; whenever they see her, they propose to her, give her love notes, ask her for recipes. Last year around Christmas, a guy who had been in for auto theft stopped by after he got out and offered Iris twenty dollars to make him a batch of her raspberry-lemon scones.

She slices mushrooms and green onions like a Japanese chef and in that jangly voice of hers sings one of the hip-hop songs she listens to on the radio. These songs are full of sexual innuendo and downright vulgarity and she sings them in the sweet, thoughtless way a child sings a nursery rhyme. She is two years younger than Tormey, and like him, is as physically healthy as any retirement-age person could hope to be.

We get the food on the table and I attempt to make a speech about the renewal of spring and the changing of seasons, but Hugh keeps interrupting me, asking if he can say grace. Hugh is forty-three, not an inch over five feet, and has huge veiny ears. He is not senile like the other two, but has been slightly out of his mind since birth. He can tell you all the moons of Jupiter, but has trouble tying his own shoes.

"May I please say grace?" he says for the third time.

I give up on my speech and we bow our heads and wait for a few seconds. Instead of saying a prayer, Hugh says the word "grace" very loudly. It takes me a minute to understand the joke and Hugh starts giggling and I laugh too until Hugh cackles so hard he falls off the back of the stool and bangs his head on the radiator. Iris stands up and says, "Oh my God he's dead." Tormey doesn't budge, keeps his head bowed, his eyes squeezed shut.

I help the little guy up and inspect the back of his head. There is just a small goose egg forming.

"He's not dead?" Iris says. She seems disappointed.

I set Hugh back on his stool and ask him if he's okay. He says, "I've got a skull like a safe deposit box."

I tap Tormey on the shoulder to inform him he can begin eating and he goes to work sucking the innards out of a stuffed pepper. The blow seems to have cleared Hugh's head a little, wiped away some of the cobwebs, and he and I spend the rest of the dinner having a detailed discussion about the political and social effects of the Viet Nam war.

Hugh, Iris and Tormey are not their real names. When we all met that first day and I found out their names were Dave, Sue and Dave—painfully common and therefore boring ones, in my opinion—I went to Garret's Used Books and bought a paperback: *20,001 Names for Baby*. I thought giving them nicknames might help them gain a fresh perspective, a new lease. I wanted them to feel this was a new beginning rather than another stop down the line. Both Iris and Tormey had spent their later years in old folks homes and with relatives who didn't really want them, and Hugh, an orphan, had spent his entire existence shuffled along, put up with, unloved. When I proposed my idea about taking on nicknames, they shrugged and said okay, as if I was asking them about switching toilet paper brands.

We spent an evening going through the book trying out names. Hugh had his heart set on Maximilian, but I convinced him that Hugh, which means "intelligence," was not only more simple and dignified, but much easier to say. Tormey told me anything was good enough for him, so I decided on his name because it is one I've never heard before and I like the meaning listed in the book: "thunder spirit." Iris's only wish was to be named after a flower.

We don't get much into their pasts; they tell me about theirs if they want to and sometimes I tell them about mine. I have thick files on each of them that I never bother looking at; I'm not a doctor or a psychiatrist, I'm just here to help out, keep things under control. We get to know each other the honest, old-fashioned way: plain old conversation.

Tormey is a little difficult because he doesn't like to talk much. All I really know about him is that he grew up on a sheep farm in Oklahoma. His arms and chest are covered with dozens of white, irregular scars. I asked him about them and he told me he got them in a war, he couldn't remember which one. He has the habit of being quiet for long periods of time, then suddenly letting loose some terrible secret or memory from his past. He catches you unawares with these sometimes ghastly, sometimes heartbreaking pieces of himself, delivering them like blows to the gut. Usually after such an occasion it takes me hours to recover, to function normally again.

I can remember once down by the creek, gathering kindling for the fireplace, when out of nowhere he turned to me, his eyes exceptionally clear and said, "I killed my son."

"What?" I said.

"I killed my baby boy. Smothered him in his crib with a piece of plastic."

"You did not."

"You're such a coward," he said to me, turned away and walked slowly, deliberate as falling snow, back towards the house.

I meet Ansie at The Dive for billiards and dinner and when she sees Hugh at my side, she looks at me with this suspicious face, her mouth and eyes forming a silent question.

Hugh is wearing a white safety helmet, something he will not venture into public without. When he's not concentrating, he has the tendency to lose his equilibrium. With his head crammed into what amounts to a shiny bowl with straps, and his big ears sticking out from underneath it, he looks like a being from another world.

I try to explain. "He was watching *Salem's Lot* on cable and it spooked him so much he was dead certain that if I left vampires would take over the house. When I got out to my car, he was already strapped in, ready to go."

"Alright," Ansie says, "no big thing," but the sideways look she's giving me says otherwise.

Tonight The Dive is doing good business. On our way to the tables, the boys at the bar, most of them loggers and Forest Service workers, slap hands with Hugh and pat his helmet. They all know him from his window and floor-cleaning job at the post office. He says, "Hey, Bub," to every one of them.

We get a corner booth. Hugh sits next to me, his head just above the level of the table.

"How was your dinner last night?" Ansie says.

"Magnificent. Better if you had come."

Ansie shrugs. She knows I'm trying to make her feel guilty. She told me that guilt is no longer in the repertoire of her emotions. She said that her five failed marriages have something to do with this. Tonight her hair is up in a shimmering blue-black bun and she smells like a women's magazine. She has a tiny brown face and big white teeth that surprise you when she smiles. We order our dinners and she tells me about the new rifle she bought. She's hoping to make the draw for the special black-bear hunt next fall. She wants to get her picture in one of those hunting magazines, kneeling next to the corpse of a bear, holding up its head so that the terrible curve of its teeth is visible.

Hugh, who usually doesn't pay attention to anything that's said unless he's being directly addressed, says, "If we could just kill all the bears we wouldn't have to worry about them anymore."

"You don't like bears?" Ansie says.

"Hate 'em. They have organisms living in their fur. When they maul you they always go right for the head. They like the way it feels when your skull snaps. For them, it's the most satisfying thing they can do."

"How do you know all this?" says Ansie.

Hugh shrugs. "People know things."

"No bear is going to maul me. That's why I bought a thirty-ought-six."

"I hope you blow their guts out," Hugh says.

It gladdens me to see these two getting along.

When the food comes, Hugh puts all his concentration into picking the bits of oregano out of his spaghetti sauce, and Ansie and I continue our conversation. We talk a lot about our ex-marriages. With five to her credit, she can go on forever. I can claim only one previous marriage and that one lasted less than a year. Talking about it with Ansie, it seems I've squeezed just about all the juice out of it I can, but she wants more, every last detail. She says the mysteries behind a broken marriage can take years to comprehend.

Speaking of my ex-wife Molly, she asks, "Now did she ever get strange telephone calls in the middle of the day? Comb your memory. Did you ever hear her whispering on the phone? This is important."

"What?"

"Just try to remember. Take your time."

Ansie doesn't believe what I keep telling her about my eight-month marriage with Molly: we broke up because we wanted different things. I wanted a family, camping in the backyard, little league games, taking the station wagon to the drive-in—the basic, boring, all-American stuff. I wanted to go to my office job someday, hangdog and bleary-eyed, and explain to my co-workers that I'd been up all night with a teething baby. Molly had other things in mind: parties, tours of Europe, a cabin at Tahoe. She had this impossible theory that we shouldn't have kids until we already had enough money saved to see each kid from infanthood through college. Somehow, we talked only vaguely about these things before-hand; we spent most of our engagement giving each other stupid presents and trying to decide where to go on our hon-eymoon. It didn't take long for us to realize that things weren't going to work. We discussed it like civilized people, shook hands, and that was the end of it. Ansie simply can't buy this. In all her considerable experience, marriages do not end with logical decisions, with the shaking of hands. They go down like burning buildings in the pyrotechnics of jealousy and drunkenness, yelling and infidelity, threats and thrown objects. You wouldn't believe some of the stories this woman has to tell.

"She wasn't having an affair," I say. "We were only married eight months for chrissakes."

"Oh, ho," she says. "My second was out testing the waters after only a few weeks."

Ansie wears her marriages like Purple Hearts.

We get down to eating, and in between bites of tortellini, she gives me a few of the sordid particulars of marriage number four that I haven't heard yet. I've known her five months and as far as her history of relationships is concerned, I think we've only scratched the surface. The saga she is relat-ing to me now, the one about one of her ex-husband's attempts to drain a swamp in Texas and make it into a reptile farm, could be made into a miniseries.

"His big seller was going to be boas," she says.

"I adore these moments," Hugh says.

"Who buys snakes?" I wonder.

"Fucking A," Hugh says. He's finished off his spaghetti and is peering through one of the holes in the top of the sugar bottle.

"Is there something wrong?" Ansie says.

"I could sure use some aerobics," Hugh says.

"I think he wants to go home," I tell her. "He gets like this."

"What about pool? We were going to go double or nothing on that fifty dollars I owe you. I can't live my life with fifty dollars hanging over my head."

"That's ideology," says Hugh.

"You want to play some pool, Hugh?" I say in my enthusiastic, come-on-old-buddy voice. "What do you say about a little eight-ball?"

This time he doesn't say anything, just continues eyeballing the sugar, his hands twitching nervously.

"He wants to go home," I say.

"Well, damn," says Ansie.

"You got that right," Hugh says.

I put my arm around him to calm him down. "Tomorrow night, okay?" I say to Ansie. "Just you and me, head to head, nobody else but the two of us."

During the day Iris is a joy to have around. She hums and waters the plants and sometimes bakes a pie or a batch of muffins. But a few times a week, at night when she's asleep, something goes wrong inside her. Her room is right above mine and I'll wake up to the muffled screech of bedsprings and a mournful wailing that goes loud and soft, loud and soft, like an air raid siren. I'll hustle up the stairs and she'll be in on her bed asleep, twisted in the sheets and producing this unearthly keening that sounds like something from a horror movie. I've set up aluminum rails around the bed so she won't fall off and snap one of her bones, and she's usually holding onto the rails with both hands, shaking them like someone clamoring to get out of jail, her translucent skin electric in the moonlight. When I take the rail off and sit next to her, she'll latch on to me, grabbing a hand or an arm with way too much strength for such a fragile body, and I'll try to shake her awake but usually she won't come out of it; she'll be somewhere way off, a place it takes awhile to get back from. I've found that picking her up and rocking her slowly in my arms calms her down better than anything. She doesn't weigh more than eighty pounds and it's like she's made of papier mâché—what a hypnotic feeling, holding another human being in your arms while they sleep, rocking them in the dark. Once she stops wailing completely, she wakes up, muttering and lost, and I'll lay her down and she'll be back to sleep within seconds. In the morning she won't remember a thing.

I'm almost never able to get to sleep after one of these occasions so I'll just stay in her room, sitting in her cherry wood rocker, listening to the soft pulse of her breathing. Simply being in her presence, innocent and unaware as it might be, gives me a full, settled feeling, the opposite of loneliness.

Ansie has just finished drubbing me in eight-ball and we're sitting in her truck outside my house, listening to a pack of ravens squawking in the shadows of an old elm down by the river. Mrs. Loder, the woman I pay to look after things when I'm out, is watching television in the front room where pieces of colored light skitter across the glass of the bay window.

I walked into The Dive fifty dollars on the plus side tonight and now I'm two hundred down. Ansie was unconscious, she could have made Willie Mosconi look like a pissant. For some reason it seems that all this success on the pool table has saddened her. She has both elbows and her forehead pushing against the steering wheel as if she intends to shove the whole steering column into the engine block. Her new gun is in the rack behind our heads, displayed in the back window like a menacing work of art.

"I don't know what I want," she says.

She is hitting on another of our favorite topics: our reluctant advance into middle age, our loss of direction and desire. I'd like to come up with something consoling or wise to say to her, but I have nothing except the trite clichés you hear in the movies time and time again.

"I used to want everything," she says. "You name it, I wanted it. That was enough for me, it was all I could handle."

I haven't seen her like this before. When we talk to each other, even about our failings, she always laughs and shakes her head, smiling, as if we're talking about one of those ridiculous soap operas on TV.

The only other truly solemn conversation I can remember us having was the first time we met. It was at a Labor Day celebration at the city park, and we ended up sitting together on a picnic table, both of us a little drunk, waiting for the fireworks to start. After a half-hour of chitchat, she suddenly announced that before we proceeded any further she wanted to get something out of the way: she had been married five times and was unable to bear children. This kind of confession from a woman I hardly knew made me feel somehow responsible to come up with a few intimate revelations of my own. I told her about my parents who resent me, their only living child, for not providing them with any grandchildren. I even told her about my brother Aaron who died just a few days after birth, how he shows up as an adult in my dreams from time to time, driving around naked in a convertible, gleeful and blowing on a long silver trumpet, yelling at me that I'm missing all the fun. We laughed about that—huge, engulfing laughs like sobs—and we've never gotten dramatically somber and serious with each other since.

"What about you?" she says now, fiddling with a knob on the radio. "Talk, say something."

"I used to want to play point guard for the Celtics," I say. "I was a hell of a dribbler at one time."

Ansie grunts and socks me on the shoulder, hard enough to leave a small knot of pain.

"Let's go inside," I say. "Have some coffee or something."

Ansie drags her fingers through her hair and looks at me. It's too dark to read her expression.

"It's late," I say. "I'm sure nobody's up there except Mrs. Loder. How can we call this a friendship when you won't even come into my house? I try to visit yours on a regular basis. What are you going to make me do, drag you in there?"

"Technically," she says, "this is not your house."

She wants an argument, a reason to stay in the truck, but I won't give her one. I get out and head for the house. "Come on," I say from the front steps. "Don't be a coward."

Mrs. Loder, a logger's wife who lives in a tiny trailer with her massive husband and three sons and consequently loves coming over any time she can, meets me at the door with a sleep-pressed face. Her hair looks like something that jumped out of the weeds and attacked her. She shuffles out to her car and Ansie steps inside, looking around, rubbing her hands nervously.

Ansie follows me up the stairs to check on everyone; it's clear she doesn't want to be left alone in this house. We look in on Iris first, and tonight it appears she has been blessed with sweet dreams or no dreams at all; against the blue-white pillowcase her face looks serene, smooth, almost youthful. Next is Tormey and he's ramrod straight under the covers, like a long-dead Egyptian king. When we poke our heads in the door he says, "Boo." Tormey simply doesn't sleep. He wanders the house most of the night, his old muscles creaking and popping like worn-out rubber bands and once in awhile it seems, like now, he climbs into bed just for old time's sake. He's up and dressed at the kitchen table by four o'clock every morning, waiting for one more sunrise. His watery eyes twinkle at us when he says good night.

Hugh is not in his bed and we find him asleep in the closet, burrowed under a pile of shoes, driven there by who-knows-what, maybe nightmares of bears coming out of the woods to gnaw on his skull. He wakes up halfway, saying that he's thirsty, and Ansie goes to get him a drink of water while I put him back to bed. His eyes still closed, he takes the glass and pours the whole thing on his face. He sputters and coughs and goes right back to sleep, his face mashed into the sodden pillow, mumbling something about the wide open sea.

I make some coffee and we sit at the kitchen table and shoot the bull. The sadness that hung around Ansie out in the truck gradually falls away and I listen to another of her marriage-slash-war stories until Tormey shows up in his suit and tie, reminding us how late it is.

We are going to the Grand Canyon. I have never had spring fever like this. I feel like I just have to *go*, it doesn't matter where. Yesterday morning I went out into the aspens and started running full tilt through the underbrush, dodging trees like a halfback, bounding over stumps, branches whipping me in the face. My lungs were on fire, my legs like jelly when I tripped on something and fell against an old slash pile, getting a long, jagged scratch on my belly in the process. God, did it feel good.

Except for Tormey, we are all natives of Arizona and none of us has ever been to the Grand Canyon. At least Hugh and Iris have no memory of ever visiting the place. It's amazing, really: one of the seven natural wonders of the world and I've never gotten up off my ass long enough to go have a look.

We'll drive up this morning, stay the night at a motel somewhere and come back tomorrow. We've got the back of the Subaru packed with a cooler of food, overnight bags and a whole toiletry case full of everyone's medication. They all seem a little giddy, like kids going off to camp. I asked them and nobody could recall the last time they took a trip. Hugh says he thinks he might have gone to Detroit one time, but he's not sure.

We drive into town and stop in front of Ansie's tiny Roadside Craft and Jewelry store. I blast through the front door, making a surprise entrance, like the Nazi SS in the movies. Ansie is on the other side of the counter gluing little colored beads on strips of leather and Gogo gives me the hairy eyeball from behind a piece of petrified wood.

"Come on," I shout. "Close up shop. We're headed for the Canyon. All you need is a camera and some fresh underwear. We'll provide the rest."

Ansie is looking out the window where Tormey is on the other side of the car, relieving his faulty bladder on a cactus.

"Holy Jesus," she says.

"Look," I say. "I haven't seen any tourists around here in days. We'll be back tomorrow. You won't be losing any business. You don't come and you'll regret it."

I go past her, back into her bedroom. I open the top drawers of her dresser.

"Where are you going?" she says, following me.

"*We* are going," I say, throwing a purple brassiere and matching panties at her. I'm brazen, I don't remember doing anything like this before; it's like this balmy weather has burned all the shame right out of me. "We are going to the Grand Canyon. Get a bag to put this stuff in. Get some tennis shoes. We might do some walking around."

"Wait, wait," she says.

Throwing more clothes on the bed, I say, "Hurry. We've got to get going. No time to lose."

Before she knows what's happened, she's buckled in, heading north on 260. We've got the windows rolled down, our faces pressed against the sharp breeze. Gogo's ears are whipping like dish towels on a clothesline.

About five miles out of Payson, Ansie looks over at me and says, "Shit, you." She's been bamboozled and she knows it. I can tell by the changing expressions on her face that she doesn't know whether to laugh or be pissed off. Just ahead of us a single doe springs across the road and vaults, at least eight feet in the air, her hindquarters a flash of white against the blue shadows, over a barbed-wire fence and into the trees.

"That was one lively horse," Tormey says.

We have the road pretty much to ourselves; every few miles a car or truck comes in a gathering rush and is gone, leaving us as we were before, the owners of the road. The big, blank sky, the pines turning to cedar and juniper as we come down out of the high country, the tiny yellow butterflies careening in the brush—all of it, ours. Iris teaches us a few lines from one of her favorite songs, "You Got One Big Thang" and we rap it together with Ansie providing the percussion by slapping the dashboard.

Less than an hour into the trip Hugh starts worrying out loud that his seat belt is too tight and could disrupt the process of his digestion and Tormey announces that he thinks he might have wet himself. Not to be left out, Iris tells us that she wants to go nowhere near the Grand Canyon, that if it's all the same to us she'll just wait in the car. "I've not come this far," she says, "to end up falling in a big hole."

Ansie turns around and helps Hugh with his seat belt, checks out Tormey who was only imagining he'd wet his pants, and tells Iris that she doesn't have to go anywhere she doesn't want and that she might just stay in the car with her. I act like I'm completely absorbed with driving and let her take care of everything. She seems a natural at this. She helps Tormey take his gout medicine and cuts up an apple and distributes the slices to everybody. "You have a fetching pair of knockers," Hugh points out as she's hanging over the seat and Ansie snorts and giggles like a schoolgirl.

About a mile out of a little town called Garner's Hope, there is a loud pop and then a grinding noise in the engine. I get out and look stupidly at the machinery under the hood. I know nothing about cars or engines, barely know how to go about changing the oil. If this were a broken condom dispenser, on the other hand, I'd have it fixed in a snap. Everyone stands behind me in the swirling dust, regarding the oil-caked motor like mourners at a funeral. "Could be a blown rod," Ansie says, "or maybe not."

"Which way should we start marching?" Hugh says.

"No marching," I say. I imagine one of them wandering out into the road, getting flattened by some hell-bent semi and my heart does a little jump-stop. I hold out my arms like a school crossing guard. "Let's get back in the car. I think this thing will start. We'll try to make it back to the town we just came out of." Ansie goes to retrieve Iris who has already strayed out into the brush to pick the tiny yellow flowers that are just budding out on the tips of the sage.

I stay on the shoulder of the road, keeping the speedometer between five and ten miles an hour, grimacing at the terrible clanking and pinging in the engine. It sounds like a crowbar loose in there. "Oh Lord," Ansie says, covering her mouth and nose, and just then the stench hits me. At first I think it's the engine, but it only takes a second to realize that Gogo, apparently spooked by the loud noise, has taken a dump under the seat. We hang our heads out the window and curse the day Gogo was ever born. Hugh, who is unlucky enough to be strapped down in the middle, holds his nose and howls indignantly.

I pull into the only gas station in town and everyone, including Gogo, bails out before I make a complete stop. The attendant, a large dusty man with a lumberjack's beard and the name *Reece* sewn in cursive on the breast of his striped jumpsuit, appears out of the tiny office and informs me that there hasn't been a mechanic in town for at least ten years. He takes a look under the hood and says, "These Japanese makes are vastly overrated, don't you think? You can use the phone to call a wrecker out of Payson."

Hugh eyes the big man distrustfully, retreating slowly, his back to the car, and says, "Don't come near me, Reece."

I sit down at the desk in the office and page through a greasy phone book, looking for numbers. I dial and look out the smokestained window of the office at the scene outside: Ansie has just finished cleaning Gogo's mess and has the cooler open, handing out sandwiches and cans of Coke. She is looking a little harried, her face polished with sweat. Hugh is fiddling with Iris' hearing aid and Tormey is sitting on the front bumper, sharing tortilla chips with Reece and Gogo. The phone ringing in my ear, I sit there watching though the dirty yellow glass that blurs my vision and it hits me that finally, in some way, I have all the things I ever wanted.

Somebody answers on the other end and not remembering

what I'm doing on the phone, I hang up and go outside. Tormey gets up and gives me a hug, crushing the bag of chips between us. Ansie holds out two sandwich bags and says, "Pastrami or ham?" I'm speechless. Everyone looks up at me and I just stand there in a puddle of oil, grinning like an idiot.

The Wig

My eight-year-old son found a wig in the garbage dumpster this morning. I walked into the kitchen, highly irritated that I couldn't make a respectable knot in my green paisley tie, and there he was at the table, eating cereal and reading the funnies, the wig pulled tightly over his head like a football helmet. The wig was a dirty bush of curly blond hair, the kind you might see on a prostitute or someone who is trying to imitate Marilyn Monroe.

I asked him where he got the wig and he told me, his mouth full of cereal. When I advised him that we don't wear things that we find in the garbage, he simply continued eating and reading as if he didn't hear me.

I wanted him to take that wig off but I couldn't ask him to

do it. I forgot all about my tie and going to work. I looked out the window where mist fell slowly on the street. I paced into the living room and back, trying not to look at my son. He ignored me. I could hear him munching cereal and rustling paper.

There was a picture, or a memory, real or imagined, that I couldn't get out of my mind: last spring, before the accident, my wife was sitting in the chair where now my son always sits. She was reading the paper to see how the Blackhawks did the night before, and her sleep-mussed hair was only slightly longer and darker than the hair of my son's wig.

I wondered if my son had a similar picture in his head, or if he had a picture at all. I watched him and he finally looked up at me but his face was blank. He went back to his reading. I walked around the table, picked him up and held him against my chest. I pressed my nose into that wig and it smelled not like the clean shampoo scent I might have been hoping for, but like old lettuce. I suppose it didn't matter at that point. My son put his smooth arms around my neck and for maybe a few seconds we were together again, the three of us.

Vernon

———————●———————

Vernon is the Arizona nobody knows about. It's ponderosa pine, blue spruce, frost on your windshield in September, elk crashing down out of the mountains in the spring. We have our fair share of old folks, but not one of them owns a recreational vehicle. We have no swimming pools! We are tan, yes, but only on our faces and arms. I've been to Phoenix a couple of times and I thought I was in hell.

These days we are down to about eight hundred souls and getting smaller all the time. Years back, the government placed restrictions on timber cutting, really putting a clamp on everything. Before that, we were something of a boom town: we had a motel and a roller skating rink and a bar with go-go dancers. This was when I was a kid and had no idea that Vernon was not the only place in the world. Now, we get hunters that stay a few days, and occasionally several tourists will wander through, take a look around and get right back in their cars and head for someplace that has a McDonald's.

I left Vernon for a semester to go to college. People around here are convinced of my intelligence. Isn't he just *smart?* they say. My mother does nothing to discourage this kind of talk. She spends a lot of her time reminding everyone what a talented guy I am, the person I could some day be if I used just a tenth of my God-given abilities. When she talks about me she uses the word *potential* a lot.

I was the valedictorian of a class of nineteen and I got a tuition scholarship to Northern Arizona. Not only that, I was the quarterback of our eight-man football team, MVP of the state championship game two years ago. In a little place like Vernon, there has to be someone everybody can throw the weight of their hopes on, and I guess for awhile, I was it.

My parents drove me to Flagstaff to help me get settled in my dorm room. When it was time to say good-bye they stood in the doorway, their faces pinched with emotion. They were holding hands, as if being on a college campus reminded them that such a thing was still possible. My roommate, who was a complete slouch, didn't have the decency to make himself scarce for a couple of minutes. "You've got big things ahead of you," I think is the line my father said that day, there in the musty dorm hall that smelled like Lysol and old sweat. Or at least it was something like that, something positively corny but also magnificent because it was coming from my old man who was so damn proud he looked like he was about to bust a vein in his head.

I liked college, liked the concept of it; I was free to do anything I wanted. Just the idea made me ridiculously happy. Like my Uncle Tim says about his first venture out into the world: it was the first time I ever got to meet people I never met before. And there were pretty girls everywhere. And beer! Every time I turned around somebody was handing me a beer. But I had this nervous feeling I couldn't get rid of, like something in the bottom of my gut slowly eating at my insides all hours of the day. I couldn't sleep. I was free to sleep until three in the afternoon if I wanted to, but the only time I could get really unconscious was in the middle of my classes. After one semester I came back to Vernon to stay.

Waylon and I hooked up in kindergarten. He taught me the dirty words he knew, I gave him the chocolate milk from my lunch; one minute we were five-year-old strangers, still the sons of our mothers, and the next we were friends for life. Who can remember what it was to be a child?

Louis (say it like the French) came later, in the third grade. His father got the foreman job at the tiny reservation-owned sawmill up by Camp Creek. Louis was an Apache, had long hair like a girl, and looked utterly bewildered out on the playground that first day. A couple of the nastier fourth-grade boys did what comes natural: they beat the hell out of the new kid. The next day a few more kids were getting ready to knock Louis around when he pulled a bayonet out of his coat. The thing was double-edged and a foot and a half long. He had stolen it from his father's collection of World War II artifacts—a Nazi infantryman's bayonet. He held it with two hands, like a sword, and he had a look in his eyes that said he wasn't going to take any more shit. What a fantastic sight: a skinny, long-haired Apache kid, letting out shrieks and war whoops and chasing around a bunch of white boys with a bayonet. In the rush to get away, Arty Lowe, one of the kids who'd helped rough him up the day before, slipped on a patch of old snow. Louis jumped on his back and rested the bayonet's point against Arty's head. The rest of us stood there, stunned and electrified. We all waited for him to skewer Arty's head like a melon, or better yet, scalp him. Instead, Louis gave him a good kick to the gut, just to let everyone know he was serious. That was enough for Waylon and me. Even though most everybody steered clear of him after that, we decided that this was somebody it wouldn't hurt to have on our side.

"Alaska," Louis says, waving a trident-shaped stick towards the north. "That should be a consideration. There's thousands of dollars in pulling the guts out of fish."

It's a week before Thanksgiving, the end of an unseasonably warm November day, and we're sitting atop Pud Mineer's woodpile, facing west where the sky is smoldering and shriveling up on itself like a burning piece of plastic. Some evenings when the air is calm and we don't want to be inside, we sit up here, each of us on a nice flat log, to discuss matters while we look out over Vernon's yards and rooftops. Up here on the lower slope of Sawtooth Peak, old Pud, a one-time rodeo clown who died in his sleep last winter, found a level spot with just enough room to put his trailer and to build up this mountain of wood. It must be thirty feet high, maybe a hundred cords; he would have had to live another eighty years just to use half this wood. Nobody ever accused Pud of being a pessimist.

"I'm not going anyplace where they charge five dollars for a gallon of milk," Waylon says, reclining on a piece of aspen, his head resting against his bunched-up jacket.

"There's a point," I say.

Louis says, "Fuck milk. I'm talking money here."

"That's exactly what I'm talking about."

"No, you're talking dairy products. Maybe you could tell us

the price of cheese and yogurt up there. That would be help-
ful. How much is a quart of eggnog?"

It seems like every week we come up with a new plan, a place
to go, a way to make money and adventure. This is one of our
favorite subjects, but talking about it hasn't gotten us far; there's
always something stopping us from leaving, some excuse or
another. I haven't said anything about the job my father called
me about a couple nights ago: an old Navy buddy of his is starting up a company that manufactures mobile homes in Oklahoma City. He plans to begin next month and would hire
anyone my father recommended, as long as they're at least
twenty-one and not members of a union. We qualify on both
accounts, with Louis, the youngest of us, having reached the
legal drinking age just last week. It's a good-paying job that
would last at least a year. I decide I won't tell them yet; I prefer
talking about job opportunities in far-off exotic places that fill
your head with the sound and color of dreams.

"There's also gold mining in Alaska," I say, trying to keep
the conversation on track.

Louis says, "I hear you can get away without paying taxes
up there."

"Maybe they'd let me get away with murder," Waylon says.

"I'd come back to haunt you," Louis grins. "My spirit will
live on forever. I'd enter a bear and bite you on the ass."

Waylon laughs and Louis whoops in the direction of the
peak and waits for an echo that doesn't come. Even though I
know this heap is as solid as the Egyptian pyramids, I have
this fear that someone is going to yell too loud or move the
wrong piece of wood, and we'll go down, buried under an
avalanche of dead juniper and pine.

We've heard a rumor that Mrs. Naegle, the ample-
breasted wife of Sheriff Naegle who lives in the adobe house
down the slope a ways, about fifty yards below us, likes to

hang out the wash and water the grass in the nude. We've been up here on at least a dozen different occasions and we've yet to see her so much as leave the house, clothed or otherwise. We don't mind waiting; all we have is time.

"You know what'd be something?" Louis says. "Light this wood on fire. In the middle of the night. Everybody'd think it was sunrise. You'd have roosters crowing and people getting up to go to work. It would be some kind of supernatural phenomenon. They'd put it on the news."

Waylon fishes around in his pocket and produces a Bic lighter. "Be my guest," he says, handing it to Louis. Louis takes the lighter, cradles it in one of his palms, smiling faintly and squinting, as if it is an object that holds great sentimental value for him. Darkness begins to gather down in the valley, rises up from deep in the woodpile to curl around our feet.

Louis puts the lighter up to his mouth and presses the button that releases the propane without igniting it. Once he's got a mouthful of gas, he purses his lips and moves his cheeks around like a wine taster. Then he opens his mouth wide, flicks a spark into it, and for a few seconds a transparent blue ball of fire hovers trembling over his tongue, a thing with a brief life of its own, making his teeth glow from within like tiny Chinese lanterns, finally collapsing on itself and guttering out with a faint popping noise.

The twelve streetlights that line Main Street suddenly come on at the same time, surprising us. Nighthawks dive and chitter over the quiet houses. All around, on every horizon, are mountains, sharp and black in the distance, holding us in like walls.

I'm the valedictorian, I get all the credit, but Waylon is the real smart one. He educated himself on the toilet. When he was a kid, he had a set of World Book encyclopedias on a shelf above the pot in the basement bathroom. He'd spend all his

spare time in there, and Frank, Waylon's father, would sometimes have to roust him out of there with a lot of threats and
door-pounding just to get him to come to dinner. Now that
Waylon is an adult and lives permanently in the basement,
he's set up a regular library in the bathroom; shelves of books
on every wall, stacked to the ceiling. He's got everything. Go
in there, pull out any three books and you'll have *The Secrets
of Oriental Sexual Massage*, *Wittgenstein: A Student's Memoir*
and *Helter Skelter*—something like that. He needs a card cat-
alogue he's got so many books in there; when I use the bathroom I can never find what I'm looking for. But I have to
admit, there is something stirring about reading Chinese
poetry while taking a dump.

Right now Waylon's into Mark Twain and I'll go over
there to visit and he'll be in on the can with that big battered
anthology on his lap, laughing to lose his teeth. He knows
electronics and gardening and transmissions, he can humiliate anyone in Trivial Pursuit or argue you into a corner with
the sheer number and heftiness of facts, but he never officially graduated from high school, never saw the point. He's big,
freckled and at the advanced age of twenty-one is already losing his curly red hair.

It's at his house that we spend most of our leisure time.
The place is always stocked with food and beer; it has a
living room big enough to play football in and girlie magazines on the coffee table. A man's house. There used to be a
woman in it, but she died a long time ago, giving birth to
Waylon. Frank keeps a small shrine to her—photographs
and letters and other memorabilia—on the mantel above the
fireplace. Even after all this time he'll squeeze Waylon
around the shoulders, a pained look on his face, and say
something like, "It's just us bozos left now. We'll have to
chin up and make do."

Like two people too close to each other, too dependent, they're always at each other's throats, always making up.

Frank is the richest man in town, that's why his house is so big. He owns the only gas station and grocery store in Vernon and owns stock in a number of corporations. He makes money like pigs make shit: it just piles up. He had a terrible fever when he was a toddler that roasted his brain a little, leaving him with slurred speech, bad eyesight and a limp. Now that he's developed a serious kidney condition that requires weekly hospital visits and a dozen different kinds of medication, he's terrified that he's going to die. Last night, we were sitting out in the front room, sipping beer, all of us a little drunk, laughing at Frank's anecdotes about what an asshole he was in high school. Suddenly he had a pain that doubled him over—he now says he knows what it feels like to be branded with a hot iron—and he pushed his fist into his left side as if there was something in there he wanted to kill. After awhile he stood up, his eyes wet, looking like he didn't know where he was.

"I'm not ready to go, godammit, nope, nope, nope," he said through his teeth, groping like a blind man for the picture of his wife on the mantel. He took it down and squeezed it so hard against his chest that the glass snapped. He gestured with the picture toward Waylon, and said to no one in particular. "I've got this knucklehead to take care of and businesses to run. And my grain shares are kicking ass."

He says one of the greatest regrets of his life was not being there when the moose showed up in his backyard. This happened just before I left for college, back when there were possibilities and expectations, when every out-of-the-ordinary thing seemed like a sign.

It was a Sunday morning after a night of Coors, potato chips and movies on the VCR. Louis was in the kitchen slurp-

ing cold cereal and me and Waylon were in on the couch waiting for a game to start on TV. Frank was out making more
money.

"There's something out there," Louis said, standing in
front of the big bay window that looks out on the back deck.
"Something big."

Frank's back yard is an unfenced piece of land that is a section of the foothills that eventually become the White Mountains. You look out there any time of the day and you're likely
to see one form of wildlife or another.

"Elk?" Waylon said.

"I don't think that's an elk," Louis said under his breath.

We went out on the deck to get a better look and God help
me if there wasn't a bull moose, antlers and all, trotting across
Frank's half-dead lawn with all the purpose of a businessman
who needed to be somewhere that very minute. None of us
had ever seen a moose in real life before and I think it took
awhile for us to figure out what we were looking at. This
thing, unlike the rather majestic moose I've seen in pictures,
appeared to have been retched up from the guts of the earth:
its burr-matted coat was fifteen of the most unsightly shades
of brown you can imagine and what looked like gray cob-
webby moss hung off its back and bowed antlers. It had
almost no neck to speak of, just an ungainly peanut-shaped
head set on top of a sagging trunk. The sheer ugliness of it was
awe-inspiring.

"That's a MOOSE!?" Louis said, in equal parts statement
and question. He had both hands jammed in his hair.

As far as I or anybody else knows, there are not supposed
to be moose in Arizona.

We watched as it ambled between a couple of apricot trees
and headed right for a life-sized foam-plastic deer Frank had
used for target practice back when he had a passion for bow-

hunting. It had been out of commission for quite awhile, but there were still about a dozen rusted aluminum arrows sticking out of it at all angles.

The moose snorted, stamped a couple of circles around the deer and gave it a few sniffs. Its penis suddenly unfurled between its legs like some hideous, searching worm. We came off the deck to get a better view just in time to see the son of a bitch mount the deer and begin humping. All this was pulled off with a complete lack of finesse or natural skill: the way it spasmed and groaned you'd think it was wounded and dying a painful death. We jumped and shouted like spectators at a boxing match but he paid no heed. For that moose, nothing else existed in the world; I mean, he was *concentrating*. We shook our fists and used every swear word we knew; this seemed to be an occasion that called for vulgarity.

"Get out of here you fucker!" Waylon cried. He was wide-eyed and indignant. I guess he didn't like the idea of this moose violating not only his father's innocent plastic deer, but the very laws of nature.

After about thirty seconds' worth of bump-and-grind, the deer began to crack and buckle and finally broke in half completely. Startled, the moose jumped back and shook his head a couple of times. He nosed the pieces of the deer and looked at us, absolutely perplexed. With his watery old man's eyes trained on us, we suddenly realized how close we were: only about thirty feet—so close we could smell him. It was a heavy, evil smell, like something rotting in a damp cave.

We put out our arms, ready to bolt, and backed up slowly toward the deck while he watched. I believe he was as surprised and baffled by this whole affair as we were. He looked around, snorted once and made for the hills, crashing through the underbrush with all the grace of a bulldozer.

Once he had disappeared, we just looked at each other, a

crazed glee rising up in our eyes. It was if we had witnessed the Virgin Mary. All the rest of that day we glowed.

After that, everywhere we went, people asked us about it. Now, more than two years later, I'm still repeating the story. Some of Vernon's more spiritually inclined believe it must be some kind of modern miracle while others say there are, without exception, no moose in Arizona (it's a fact!), especially not misshaped, rangy moose that attempt to mate with man-made objects. As far as we're concerned, it doesn't matter what anybody says. We don't care what can be confirmed or denied: we were there, we saw him, he belongs to us.

It kills Frank that he wasn't a witness to this marvel that occurred in his own back yard. He wonders why we didn't shoot the damn thing, or at least take a picture of it. I have a whole cabinet full of guns, ready for use, he says, just for occasions like this. I think he's become obsessed with it; he still talks about it all the time and occasionally he'll wander out into the hills with his binoculars hoping to see it for himself, just once. I think in some small way he identifies with that ugly, lonesome thing, with the confusion that comes with being lost in the world, fearful of what you can't understand, of all the unfamiliar country.

For a few years there were four of us, not just three. He had to have one of the worst names on record: Hyman Dimbatt. Not only was his first name part of a woman's sexual apparatus, but his last you'd use for somebody who'd poured orange juice on their corn flakes. He came to Vernon to live with his uncle's family the summer before the eighth grade. There had been problems with his family in Albuquerque that no amount of persuasion could get him to talk about.

Hymie had a great sense of humor. You'd have to, I guess, with a name like that. He was taller than the rest of us by almost a foot and walked around in an apologetic hunch. We tried to teach him to play basketball but he had no talent for it. He couldn't put the ball in the hoop from a foot away! He was a klutz and had the body of a freak but at least he was hilarious. He'd trip and dive headlong into the wall, books and pens flying everywhere, just to make you smile. When we got old enough to think we were men, we'd spend the night at Waylon's and play poker and smoke Swisher Sweets. Hymie would perform some antic Jerry Lewis hilarity and I'd laugh so hard that I once chucked up a whole night's worth of Michelob and corn chips right on the biggest pot of the night.

Hymie was with us for nearly three years. After a summer day spent hauling hay on his uncle's alfalfa field, Hymie and a couple of the wetback farmhands went to cool off at the Cannon. The Cannon was a corrugated steel culvert, about twenty yards long with a diameter of two and a half feet. It is still the only channel that regulates the irrigation water from the reservoir canal to the fields south of town. If you went at a time when the gates were up and the water was rushing out, you could sit down at the culvert's mouth in the cold roaring current and let it take you full force through sixty feet of blue darkness—your own screams slamming back in your ears—and then surging out, shot like a pea from a straw, newly born in the bright light of day, plunging ten feet, arms and legs flailing, into a foaming muddy pool. This used to be one of the sublime aspects of summer in Vernon.

Hymie was the first to go in that day, and as it turned out, the last ever. When they went to the other end and couldn't see any sign of him, the wetbacks got worried. They looked into the culvert, but the water was extremely high and all they could see was blackness. They thought maybe Hymie had played a trick on them, gone through the Cannon, gotten out of the pool and hidden behind a bush just to give them a scare. I can imagine them, their eyes wide with concern, yelling *"Hymie? Hymie? Dónde está?"* By the time they got someone who could shut the gates down, Hymie had been in there over fifteen minutes. They found his long, naked body wrapped around an ancient wooden tennis racket that had somehow become wedged crosswise in the middle of the culvert. His wristwatch was found a hundred yards away at the bottom of the ditch and his underwear out in Henderson's milo field a few days later. Nobody knows what became of his pants. For months after they put steel grates over both ends of the Cannon, you could hear parents and the older citizens around town saying how it takes someone to die for people to get serious, for precautions to be taken.

Hymie's folks showed up a day later looking pale and stricken, like war refugees, and took his body back to Albuquerque. Waylon, Louis and I went to the funeral together but the directions his uncle had given us weren't accurate and we got lost. We were sixteen, I had just received my driver's license and none of us had ever driven in a town with stop lights before. I still hadn't mastered the art of making a left turn in traffic, and we had people honking at us and giving us the finger. I got spooked and began driving like someone with no concept of what a brake or a gearshift was; I drove over medians, ran red lights and nearly had us on our way to early funerals of our own.

While Hymie was being eulogized and lowered into the earth, we were in a Winchell's asking a fat black lady for directions home.

I've just gotten off work and leaves are tumbling down on the hood of my truck. It's not evening or afternoon, but that perfect in-between time when you can see the molecules of the air. I'm not ready to go home to my empty little trailer by the reservoir, so I'm driving around, smelling the wood smoke that's trailing out of Vernon's chimneys.

I pass the house where my family lives, the house I lived in my entire life until I went to college. I park on the other side of the street, intent on going inside to say hello, maybe talk with my father about the Oklahoma job, but instead I walk around to the side of the house where Marty Isaacson, our next-door neighbor to the north, has an acre plot of corn that adjoins our property. I stand in the old brittle stalks and watch. I'm across from the kitchen window, which is situated just above the sink. The light coming out of the house is almost blinding. My mother comes into view and I step back deeper into the corn. She is washing something in the sink, talking back over her shoulder, and my father's voice is in the background, a low thrumming. He is the principal of the high school, town council chairman, always talking on the phone. Somewhere in the house I hear a toilet flush.

I have the feeling of something empty opening up inside me, an expanding hollow feeling like homesickness, here, ten yards away from my own house. With the mulberry trees out front, the smell of chicken enchiladas from inside, the splintered dent in the garage door I made coming home late one night, it's the most familiar place in the world to me, but it's not mine, not anymore. I had a good life here as a kid—so good it almost makes me feel guilty. I know I should be somewhere else, working to make my own place, busting my ass to become the successful, independent guy everybody expects, but something—a fluttering in the stomach, the weight of my own insides—keeps me where I am.

My two little brothers come out into the front yard and start playing Wiffle ball. They are supposed to be raking leaves before supper but no one is supervising, so they're working on their fastballs and sliders. They're calling each other cocksuckers, just quiet enough so no one inside can hear them. My mother turns and laughs at something. She has white, beautiful teeth.

It has become night without me realizing it and I am absolutely invisible, lost in the corn. I'm not happy or sad or anything. I stand there watching for a long time, until the air is blue-black and the cold has taken the feeling from my feet and hands.

"I don't know about that," Louis says. "Shit, I don't know. How much you say a month?"

"Two thousand minimum. With overtime you can make three and a half."

It's late and we're driving around town, cruising, in Louis' grizzled old VW Bug. I've just finished telling him about the mobile-home job my father is urging me to take. Waylon is working the late shift at the gas station, so it's just the two of us.

"We'd have to be in Oklahoma City by December first," I say.

"That's in what, ten days? That's the weekend we were going hunting."

I shrug, pick up an old, dirty *Sports Illustrated* that's among the garbage under my feet and page through it.

"You said something to Waylon?" Louis says.

"I figured I'd ask you first. We can talk to him on the way over to Payson tomorrow night."

"You going to do it?" Louis says, like he's daring me to say yes.

"It's twice what I make at the mill. The three of us could go and we'd have a party, we could roll cigarettes with five-dollar bills."

"All that money," Louis smiles. "Think of the women."

"And Albuquerque's right on the way. There's our chance to pay Hymie a visit."

Though it's been over five years since the day we couldn't find the cemetery, we've yet to go back to give it another shot, to pay Hymie our last respects. We've planned trips to see him so many times I can't count, but always, it seems, there's something getting in the way.

"Man," Louis says with a far-off look in his eyes, studying a ketchup stain on his shirt for a long time. Hymie's death seems to have affected Louis more than anyone. He won't discuss it, won't even say Hymie's name, and when I tell him this is the kind of thing he needs to talk out, he just shakes his head: no, no, no.

He spits on a paper napkin and starts rubbing the stain out of his shirt. There is no need for him to actually look at the road; we've driven these streets so many times we could do it blindfolded.

"I just have all this shit to worry about," Louis says. "You know that lawyer my pop just hired?" He goes into a long explanation about the latest news of his parents' ongoing divorce: alimony, division of property, and so on. Right now, Louis is a sort of go-between for his mother and father, and he sincerely believes that if he can manipulate everything properly, his parents will get back together. They love each other, he told me once, I just have to make them remember that.

The reasons behind the divorce everybody knows—this is a small town—and the story is quite simple: Mrs. Tilousi was making trips to Santa Fe every week or two where she was supposed to be involved with the production of a book on Native American photography, but instead, as everybody but Louis' idealist father could guess by then, was really having an affair with the photographer. Mr. Tilousi never realized that his wife, a fervent, fast-moving woman, could not be con-fined in a tiny place like Vernon. I remember spending the night at Louis' once when I got up to go to the bathroom, and there she was, alone in the front room, looking out the win-dow, dancing to an old Sinatra song and kissing her own hand.

On the other side of the coin Mr. Tilousi is the nicest, most unassuming man on earth, and that was a big part of the prob-lem. That he saw action in Viet Nam does nothing to change this. He is anything but one of those ex-soldiers with vulgar tattoos on his biceps and too many stories to tell. He is the type of veteran who, even after everything, still believes in the shining ideals that only the truly stubborn can hold onto—obligation, loyalty and trust. When Mrs. Tilousi failed to come back from one of her excursions, he was the last to understand that his wife had run out on him.

Louis parks the car under Turnback Bridge, next to the river. Vernon is dead quiet around us; the only sound is water moving through the dead reeds, rustling them like paper. I start to get out to take a piss, but Louis touches my arm and begins talking again in a rush of words, everything blurted out a little too loud as if it is something he wants to hold back, but can't. Speaking of the day the photographer took his mother away for good, he says, "Shit, you know, I thought it was just another one of their trips. I was helping load her things in this asshole's car and there was one of those metal photographer's briefcases in the guy's trunk and I opened it up to check out what kind of equipment he had. There were a bunch of black and white pictures in there of a naked woman—legs spread, butt in the air, that kind of thing."

Louis stares into the lights of the control board and his fin-gers pop the cigarette lighter in and out. "I started getting horny until I realized the woman was my mom."

I look at my reflection in the windshield. The moon has just come up and there are pieces of it floating in the river. Louis gets out and stands away from the car in the tall weeds, as if he can't stand to be anywhere near the ghosts of the words he just said.

Sometimes we like to relive the glory days. After work and supper on a calm evening we'll go round up a few high school boys and drive out to the football field for a pick-up game of night football. We won the state championship our senior year, the only time a Vernon team has even come close to doing something like that.

Gart Higgins, the school custodian, won't turn on the field lights for us anymore ever since the school district got an unaccountable extra three hundred dollars on its electric bill, but we have the next best thing: a glow-in-the-dark football that Waylon ordered from a novelty magazine. It's hollow, made of hard, thin plastic, and has a clear tube through the middle in which you insert a green glo-stick. You might think something like this would be hard to play with, but it's weighted just right, takes a tight spiral and the holes in it make it easy to grip. In the dark, green rays of light shoot out of it like something from a science fiction movie—a huge egg out of which an alien baby is about to come forth.

We divide the teams and dig in. What is there to say about adrenaline in your veins, the smell of grass, a ball like a spiraling star against the black, bug-filled air? For me it is beauty or art, something better than life. The dim, grunting bodies on the dark field, the sound of your own feet pounding the turf, the hollering and cussing that comes from deep down, the green, liquid light of the ball above you as you dive to catch it, early dew spraying your face as you slide to a stop in the long grass. Have you ever collided with someone so hard you feel no pain whatsoever, only a warm, pleasant buzz? There's something to that. There's something to putting it on the line in a pitch-dark, deserted place where nobody watches.

When we've had enough we sit around on our tailgates and talk about this hit or that catch or who might be getting a piece of ass this weekend. Maybe we rib the high school boys for what a shitty team they are fielding this year. It's on nights like this we are powerful and unafraid, and we can drive off separately into the night, alone, satisfied, and wake up the next morning with a sweet ache sitting in our bones like a memory.

The lack of viable women in Vernon is heartbreaking. The young ones are either gone, married or pregnant. There are a few older single ladies, but these scare me: they have husky voices and are the hardened leftovers from a generation gone by. The most famous of this group is Ginny Whurt, a red-haired woman in her forties who drives around in a long, avocado-green Plymouth, propositioning men from the car window. She makes no distinctions; she's been known to sit out in front of the junior high school and ask the boys coming out if they wouldn't like a nice blow job. We don't really mind having her around—she makes the place a little more interesting and provides a release for those desperate souls who really have a need.

So: we must go elsewhere to find feminine affection. We get on the old, cracked highways toward Round Valley, Holbrook or Snowflake, wind in our hair and anticipation taking the spit out of our mouths. Usually we end up walking the empty streets or sitting in bars watching pretenders in cowboy hats dancing with the pretty ones. Lord, what long drives those are, coming home failures, like the wounded from a lost war.

Last night was one of our few successes: a trio of girls from Ohio with a yearning to match ours. They were making a tour of the great Southwest and we ran into them at the county fair in Payson.

In the truck on the way to Payson, Louis and I presented Waylon with the possibility of the mobile-home job. As we discussed it, I tried to talk it up, whip up some enthusiasm; when it comes to topics like this, Waylon and Louis look to me because I am the one who went off alone to college, because, except for Hymie, I'm the only one of us who has ever ventured out into the unknown.

After some serious deliberation, we decided we were definitely going to do it, we needed to get away from Vernon where some real money could be made. Then Waylon started mumbling that he didn't think he would be able to leave that soon, there were a lot of things he needed to take care of before he could just take off, and suddenly Louis chimed in about all the problems with his parents, and if he was going to quit his job he had to give at least two weeks' notice, and so on and so forth. With my heart constricting in my chest, I started shouting at them, I couldn't help it. *Fucking cowards*! I yelled at them. *Candyasses*! Louis punched the dashboard and told me to shut up. We drove the rest of the way in silence.

Meeting that Midwestern trio, however, instantly cleared our minds of doubt and hard decisions, made us forget about anything that wasn't soft, curved, perfumed and right there in front of our faces. When one of them started stroking Louis' braids, asking him if being an Indian didn't give him any special abilities, I knew things would go well for us. It didn't take long for us to pair off to private places and after one of the best nights of our lives, with the sun just over the trees, we made a dramatic scene of saying good-bye forever to those sweet girls and got in the truck, feeling flat-out content with ourselves;

the bubbling, silvery gas of success filled our heads and we pretty much floated back to Vernon.

By the time we dropped Waylon off at his house it was ten o'clock in the morning, four hours after he should have been to work at Frank's store. Making things worse was the fact that Waylon, his brain seized up with hormones, had forgotten to call Frank and tell him he wouldn't be home until morning. Frank is forever worrying about Waylon's well-being, and when Waylon is away without Frank knowing where he is, even for just awhile, Frank gets completely bent out of shape.

When we drove up Frank was out in the front yard digging up a dead fruit tree. "Shit, shit, shit," Waylon said before he got out of the truck.

He tried to make it to the front door, but Frank blocked his way, his thick glasses catching the sun. "What the hell?" Frank said.

Waylon mumbled something at the ground.

"What?" Frank said.

"Nothing," said Waylon.

Frank grabbed Waylon around the back of the neck, the way you would a kid who's done something naughty. Now, Frank is a big man, but not as big as his son. To get his hand on Waylon's neck he had to reach *up*. Waylon tried to push him away, Frank cuffed him on the side of the head and they went at each other. They wrestled around for a minute, vying for leverage, then stood toe to toe, hitting each other point blank like two big hockey players producing the time-honored crack and slap of meat and bone. God, how they loved each other! Frank gave up at least four inches and seventy pounds, but he held his own; he must have the skull of a rhino. His glasses had been knocked off and his eyes were like two puckered holes with nothing in them, but he kept flailing away, not giving an inch. Waylon reared back and delivered a stiff right cross that laid his father out. Holding his head in his knobby, scraped hands, Frank got up and said in the strained voice of someone who has just downed a glass of vodka, "Holy Jesus what a shot!" He was proud of his boy, but he wasn't giving up. He dived in for more and Waylon, tears dripping off his nose, grabbed Frank around the chest in a bear hug and pulled him to the ground. They lay there in the dirt, like survivors of a car crash thrown clear of the wreckage, locked in a desperate clinch, all the heat and blood gone out of their faces, not wanting to hurt each other any more than they already had.

We are jammed together in the front seat of Louis' Bug, on the way to Haight's Peak, climbing toward the sun, doing our best to get ourselves out of the rut we've been in much too long. It's the last day of the hunt and all three of us have yet to bag a deer. Nothing like this has ever happened before; we've always got our kills in the first couple weeks of the season when the big bucks still have the green music of summer on their minds and don't expect what's coming. This fall we've had our distractions: Louis' parents' ongoing divorce, Frank's kidney problems, and lately the prospect of this mobile-home job.

Over the past week since our trip to Payson, we've done nothing but argue about whether or not we should take off and head for Oklahoma City. Two nights ago, just twelve hours before we would have had to leave town to arrive there by the December first deadline, we were at a booth in the Alpine Diner, the only sit-down eatery in Vernon, nibbling chicken wings and watching the TV over the bar. After arguing and agonizing and writing the pros and cons down on a grease-stained napkin, we had almost convinced ourselves that, yes, we were going to do it, we were going to hop in our vehicles the next morning and head east toward the rising sun, out into the wide open spaces—when the weather report came on the television: severe weather for at least the next three days, travel advisories for all southern Rocky Mountain states. We didn't look at each other or speak; a weatherman with swirled acrylic hair talking about wind speeds and icy roads was all it took to destroy what little momentum we had built up for ourselves. In one instant we gave up altogether on Oklahoma City, on piles of money and all the happiness it could buy us, on stopping off in Albuquerque to visit Hymie's grave.

I didn't—couldn't—say anything. I wanted to scream, shout myself ragged, but I didn't have the strength even to mumble a cussword; it was like I had been paralyzed by the dark things grinding inside me—fear, shame, anger—all tangling together in the pit of my gut like a wad of junk metal.

We sat limp at that booth for awhile, all the air gone out of us, and finally, when we were able to haul ourselves up and go outside, there were already tiny crystals of snow falling, ticking on the hood of my truck. We talked for a few minutes, whispering, never looking each other in the eye, and decided that if we weren't going to Oklahoma City, the very least we could do is go get our deer. It's an embarrassment to anybody who doesn't get their deer in a season—not only that, it's considered a bad sign for things to come. But the weather has been even worse than expected: in the past two days there have been windstorms, snow flurries, some rain, some lightning, a little of everything. We even had to give up on our idea of the last-ditch hunt. I stayed home in bed (I had taken the days off from work) and listened to the wind rattling my walls, making my trailer shake and shimmy like an old boxcar going too fast on a ruined track. After the wind bawling in my ears all last night, I woke up this morning to Louis poking me in the ribs, telling me to get my boots and gun, we were going hunting. Feeling like somebody raised from the dead, I walked out into a world so calm it spooked me.

We did nothing to prepare for the hunt, just jumped in Louis' car and now, because the back seat is full of old engine parts, I'm stuck between Louis and Waylon in the front seat. I do what I can to keep from being seriously injured by the gearshift between my legs.

"Do you think Haight's Peak is under eight thousand feet?" Waylon says. "The book I was reading says it's a rare moose that will go much higher than that."

Forget bagging a deer, Waylon is intent on bringing home our famous moose, not only to prove the unbelievers wrong, but as a birthday present for Frank, who turns fifty-eight next week.

"I just want to kill something," Louis says. "Anything."

I keep quiet; I'm trying to enjoy the hush of the air in the trees, the flat, empty sky. The narrow road we're on is littered with broken branches that crunch and jump up when we pass over. Every second we're moving higher and higher to a place where the air is so sharp and clean it can make you forget who you are.

Just after we've passed the Fancy Springs turnoff, Louis throws on the brakes and says, "Shit!" and gets out. There is a young ponderosa, about as thick as a telephone pole, lying across the road. I give it a kick and find that it's heavy enough to make my toes smart. If we had my truck, we could use the chainsaw I keep in my utility box and be on our way, but my truck is at Clay's garage, getting the front end fixed. Early Saturday morning with the storm moving in from all directions, just a few hours after we'd parted ways at the Alpine Diner, Sheriff Naegle caught me weaving down Main Street with an empty pint of Wild Turkey and the dents from the stop sign I'd run over all too evident on my front bumper. I can't remember any of this, but it made it to the front page of the weekly paper that came out yesterday: an embarrassment to everyone. But just as embarrassing is going hunting in a piece of shit like this.

It's pitiful, really, but what can we do? We mill around, cussing under our breaths, trying to think. Waylon is not to be deterred: he assumes a squatting position, places his hands under the front bumper, gives himself a short pep-talk and lifts. He actually gets it three or four inches off the ground, the freckles on his face turning white against his red skin, and he hisses at us, "Are you going to stand there and LOOK?" We hustle over to help him pull the front tires over the tree, and while Waylon holds up the front end, Louis and I, with a lot of groaning and yelling, lift the back end over so that the car, with its delicate oil pan and muffler, does not even graze the tree's rough bark.

You lift a car over a tree (even a small foreign car) and for a time you feel capable of pretty much anything. Two miles up the road we have to go through the procedure again, only this time with a slightly bigger tree, and it takes so much exertion I feel like at any second my intestines are going to fly out of my ass like paper streamers.

By the time we make it to the turnoff, we have about five hours of daylight left, just enough time to make the circle around Mount Baldy and back. This is a place where we've had a lot of luck before, but today it's quiet and empty, as if the rain washed all life right off the mountain and into the rivers. We skid over the slick clay and listen to the sound of hope crumbling to dust inside us; there is no deer sign at all—no tracks or scat or fur left on the side of a tree by a rutting buck, and certainly no indication that a moose has ever been here—

only the weird, clean stillness cracked once in awhile by the tired shriek of a bird.

In our hurry to make it up here we forgot everything but our guns and ammunition. Instead of camouflage I'm wearing a sweatshirt that says "Stanford" in bright neon yellow, something my mother bought me back before she had lost all hope too. After awhile there doesn't seem to be any point in stepping quietly or keeping our guns up and ready. When we slip and fall on our asses we don't even bother cussing. We trudge along silent and shamefaced, as if the lack of life on this mountain is something we are responsible for.

The sun is just above the treeline when we make it back to the road, covered to our armpits in mud. The car is about a mile down the road, which at this point seems too, too far. We walk no more than a hundred yards, come around a sharp curve and there before us, a gift: a hundred and fifty yards away down in a tiny meadow, four bucks walking lazily together, their brown backs sleek and shiny in the dull yellow grass. It's what they call a bachelor group—young males, not yet ready, like the older, seasoned bucks, to go it alone in the higher elevations where the air is thinner and the footing not as sure. There is no wind to speak of and they are aware of nothing but themselves.

This is as easy as it gets, as easy as falling off a chair. We fire at the same time, a single *snap!* that loses its sharpness and turns into the sound of dense static as it echoes away. Two of the bucks drop instantly as if something has fallen on them from out of the sky and the two others hightail it in opposite directions, diving into the underbrush. We forgot to decide who was shooting which deer before we fired, but that doesn't matter, we've been smiled upon by God or Mother Nature or whoever it is that controls things around here—we got two bucks in the dying minutes of the hunt. Louis goes running down the slope to see what we've come up with, his hair flowing behind him like a banner.

It's dark by the time Waylon brings the car back and we get the carcasses up on the road. We're whooping and shouting and clapping each other on the back. We got a two- and a four-pointer, both in the area of two hundred pounds, and what's more, we made good hits; they were both dead before they knew their numbers had been called. A small breeze comes up and I can already smell the steaks cooking. It's too dark and we don't have any of the necessary equipment to gut and dress them, not even a pocketknife, so we throw them on top of Louis' car, blood, guts and all. Because we didn't bring rope, we have to lash them on as best we can with our shoelaces.

We stuff ourselves back into the car and coast down through the tight looping curves, the pine-scented air swirling in our heads. We are dirty and exhilarated and when we have to get out to lift the car over the downed trees, even with the extra four hundred pounds on top, it's like we're lifting a baby carriage—we're that happy. Blood is running steadily down all the windows and dripping through the rust holes in the roof and we're belting out Jimmy Buffet's "I Wish I Had a Pencil-Thin Mustache." This is our favorite song and we reserve it for special occasions like this one. We put our *souls* into it. Waylon appears to have forgotten all about the moose and Louis has the wipers going and he's hunched over the steering wheel, squinting to see through the streaked glass and yodeling his heart out. With the glow from our headlights coming through the blood-washed windshield everything inside the car has turned a fresh-meat pink. We are crammed together, almost on top of each other, covered with mud and sweat and blood—we are a singing pile of carnage. Our vocal chords are gritty and raw, our lungs nearly given out, but we keep it going, hoarse and loud as we ease down the last slope out of the darkness and trees, toward the few, scattered lights of home.

.

Snake

It's the biggest snake I ever seen without the aid of liquor. Sitting there in the kitchen watching water drip in the sink, resting up after a long fight on the toilet with my constipation, when I seen it go racing down the hall to the bedrooms, probably after a mouse. My eyes are no damn good anymore, but it was a big bull snake, I guess, fat as my leg and six feet long.

Somebody's always leaving that damn screen door open. Got to pull it shut tight! I'm forever yelling at the girls. You don't keep that door shut, you got snakes racing through here, sometimes these rattlers, big ones, just looking for a shady place to choke down a mouse. Wait till somebody gets bit and the screen door's going to get shut tight every time.

"Hey-yah! Close the screen door!" Hurts my head yelling

that loud but nobody listens otherwise. Probably more snakes on their way in right now. Come right on in, snakes! I say. What's the difference between one snake in the house and three or eight snakes? At least they get the mice.

Pretty soon I get up to shut the screen door. I got some of that damn arthritis, walking from the kitchen to the porch is just about enough to kill me. It hurts so much, my knees are so bad, I have to say shit every time I put my foot down. Walking around and it's shit, shit, shit, shit, shit. Since I got the arthritis I probably said shit six hundred thousand times. Door's wide open and I guess since I'm already here it's just as good if I sit on the porch for awhile. Nobody wants to sit in a house that's got a big snake in it.

My boy Cornelius, he's out front working on his car. He probably just got back from work, usually he comes in to have something to drink after work, but he's set on getting that car fixed. The girls, they're out back, maybe, messing around like usual. Cornelius' wife, her name was Ada, lived with us until a year and a half ago when she was walking into town, it was early morning and dark, and somebody ran off the road and hit her. Killed her just like that. Christmas day and we're all sitting around wondering what's taking her so long to bring the food home. Every day Cornelius has to walk two miles into town, right past the spot Ada died (me and the girls made a little pile of rocks there to remember it) for his job working on the new tribal building. Every afternoon he walks two miles back unless there's somebody nice enough to give him a ride. Usually there's not.

Cornelius is still tore up over it. He walks right on the white line, sometimes out in the road, hoping maybe a car will come along and hit him too, take him away so he can be with Ada again. I try telling him he needs to go into town some nights and find himself a new mother for the girls but he don't like to listen to much I say. I feel bad for the girls, with only me and Cornelius to look after them.

We live down here at the south edge of the reservation, right on the highway that comes down out of Globe. We got a pretty good HUD house, better than most, with a extra room Cornelius put on last summer, and a pen with some goats and chickens. We got it all to ourselves, the sagebrush, creosote, juniper, coyotes, jackrabbits, lizards and a wild horse named Tom (the girls named him that after somebody on the TV) who comes up to the kitchen window some nights, sticks his head right in the house and makes a lot of godawful noise. I always get up, sometimes the girls too, and we give Tom a potato or some licorice or whatever we got in the house. He stands there munching whatever it is like he's thinking about something important. We had dogs too, probably a dozen of them, one time or another, but every one ran out on the highway and got wiped out by a truck or a station wagon or some old white people in a motor home. Finally we stopped getting dogs. Burying those poor dead dogs, the girls crying and carrying on, only so much of that you can take.

Out back is a wickiup I built so the girls could see what kind of house their grandfather used to live in. I'm always trying to teach them some Apache words but they don't want none of that. They just run around like rabbits, never stopping, you know, like girls do. That wickiup is their favorite place to play now. They pretend it's a castle or a shopping mall or something else like that.

"Snake in the house," I say to Cornelius and settle down on my lawn chair. "Big snake."

Cornelius has himself stuck so deep into that car it's only his ass sticking out of there. The car is some old thing, rusted up pretty bad. Cornelius bought it off Virgil Kitcheyan for fifteen dollars one night when Virgil was drunk as a rat. Looks like maybe Virgil pulled it out of a river.

"Sure hot today," I say to nobody but myself.

After a while Cornelius pulls himself out of the car, says, "There's some kind of police with his car broke up the road. He's doing a lot of cussing at his car."

"You help him?"

"Not no police I didn't."

"You hear what I said about the snake?"

Cornelius keeps his mouth shut. He won't never admit to it, but he's afraid of snakes. When there's a snake to be killed I'm the one that's got to do it.

The girls come running up from the back of the house. Charlotte, eight, and Peaches, five. Been playing in the sand-wash behind the house. Both dirty as hell and screaming like coyotes. We need to find them a mother alright.

Charlotte swats Cornelius right on the ass and Peaches wraps herself around one of his legs. They keep squealing, oh they are so happy, oh they sure do love their daddy, oh, oh, oh. They got so much energy it makes me tired. Cornelius keeps banging around inside the car and the girls sit down in the dirt to watch. Sure pretty with the sun in their hair. I got to remember to keep them away from the boys.

Cornelius jerks up out of the car and holds up a cut thumb. Just a tiny bit of blood on it, looks like. He changes his voice, like a white man's, and looks over at the girls, "You see what this car did? Damn car cut me! Ow! Oh boy, look what it done. Come on, car, you got to cooperate." He gives the car a good kick on the bumper. "This ain't funny. I'm going to light you on fire you piece-of-crap car!"

The girls squeal so hard they fall backward. They love it when their Daddy makes like a white man. Good to see Cornelius messing around like he used to.

Little Peaches starts to yelling, jumping up and down, pointing at the road. She's got crow's eyes, can see for miles. Sure enough, here comes somebody walking this way. Whoever he is, he's still far off and you can barely make him out through the heat coming up off the road.

"It's that goddamn police," Cornelius says with his thumb in his mouth. "A fat-ass white guy."

Cornelius doesn't like white people, never did, and I guess a fat white police for him would be double bad. I like to sit out front and watch the cars go by and most times it's white people driving. Sometimes they see the house with the wickiup and they stop to have a look. I guess they think the only reason we're here is for tourists to look at.

I always liked the hippies best. Them and the Jehovah's Witnesses. Some years back, hippies were all over the reservation, running around in their vans and school buses, all of them wanting to learn how to be Indian. Never made no sense, but they were nice.

I got a favorite hippie, this one showed up a few years ago. I guess he only knew one word: "Wow." He had curly red hair all over him and he had on a kind of leather loincloth, like a big dirty diaper and his big purple pecker hanging out of it. He didn't give a shit. He walked around the wickiup, went inside, came back out and he just kept saying it, "Wow."

We stood there for awhile and he went ahead and said it again, "Wow."

So I just said it right back, "Wow."

He liked that. We were best friends after that. Before he left he gave me a little paper sack with some marijuana it. Some pretty good stuff.

So now here's this police with a broke down car. He looks like he's been walking for a good long way, teetering some, lugging a briefcase like it's full of rocks. He comes walking up the path and Cornelius keeps his head stuck in the car. The girls stand and stare like they never seen a fat white man before.

He stops in front of the porch, making a sound like, huf huf huf. He's got on a tan uniform with patches on it and he's wet all over, looks like he fell in a cow trough. White people don't have no trouble sweating.

"You have a phone?" he says. Huf huf huf.

"All we got is beer," I say.

He thinks on it for a minute, his head is so red and swelled up it looks like it might pop. "That would be good, fine. Is it hot? How is it this hot? Oh Lord I'm just about to die."

I start telling Charlotte to run get a Coors, but I remember the snake. I'm pretty sure it's not a rattler, but I don't want anybody getting bit. I go inside to get the beer. Walking to the kitchen, it's the same old thing, one foot at a time, shit shit shit shit. Cornelius wanted to get me a cane but I told him somebody gives me a stick I'll just end up hitting people with it.

I give a look in the bedroom and the bathroom, but that snake's got himself hid up somewhere. I'll find him later. I get a six-pack and stick my head in the freezer for a minute to cool off some.

Been a few months since I stopped drinking. There's this lady doctor comes around every once in awhile, works for the BIA, and she told me I keep drinking my liver will go rotten, or something like that. She was a good looker, had some tits on her, and she put her hands under my shirt and down my pants, feeling things. First time in maybe ten years my pecker's got hard.

Outside Cornelius is whacking on the car extra loud and our friend has pretty much got his breath back. I get another lawn chair for this guy who's big as an outhouse and smells like flowers. When he settles down it's a miracle the chair doesn't fall to pieces. "Car broke down up the road aways," he says. "Chrysler Cordoba. This car's not two years old and it looks like the fuel pump's gone on it. My cousin Cecil sold it to me, that fucking apple. I'll tell you one thing," he takes a drink of beer, wipes his mouth. "Don't *ever* buy a Chrysler Cordoba."

He sucks his beer and sticks his hand at me. His fingers are like wet hot dogs. "Bud Anderson."

"You the police?" I say.

He laughs and I can see all kinds of metal in his teeth. The sweat is just running off him.

"Arizona Fish and Game," he points to the patch on his shoulder. "I was on my way to Phoenix to get drunk and pick up my retirement plaque. No way I'll make it now."

I tell him he might be able to hitch a ride, but he shakes his head. "I'd rather hump a cactus than stay one more minute in that sun."

I yell at Cornelius to come get a beer. He looks at me, doesn't say nothing. He's got a look on his face, angry and ashamed, like he's got something stuck up his ass but don't exactly know what to do about it. It's his I-don't-care-for-white-people face. Me, I spent some years working at the sawmill up at McNary, had to spend time with white people. Learned what they're like. But Cornelius has never been off the reservation except to go to Phoenix a few times. The only people he ever got to know was his teachers down at the Indian school.

After standing there for awhile, Cornelius comes and takes a seat on the other side of me, still holding a screwdriver. He pops open a beer with the screwdriver and drinks half of it right off. The girls get in the car and make like they're driving someplace far away from here.

"No phone, then?" Bud says.

"Just beer," I say.

Bud nods, says, "I follow you."

"Bud's not the police," I tell Cornelius.

"Happy to hear it," Cornelius says.

"He's a forest ranger," I say.

"I'll tell you what," Bud says. "I've been in worse situations than this."

The sun is going down behind us so it's starting to cool down some. Bud puts down two more beers and Cornelius starts on his second while we watch the shadows of the house stretch out toward the road. Bud's finally starting to get back some of his original color. I can't stand it no more, having two people chugging it down on both sides of me. Stop drinking for a few months and all the sudden you find out how good beer smells. I sit there and sniff their beers and it's like I'm dying of thirst. I guess I'll have one can, maybe two, not even enough to make my knees stop hurting.

"You doing a fix-it job on that Caddy?" Bud says to Cornelius.

Cornelius watches me popping open my beer, but doesn't answer Bud.

"Because if you are, I've got a guy down in the valley can get you any part you need. Some of those old Caddy parts are hard to come by these days. I think maybe I'll get myself an old Caddy. They knew how to make a quality car at one time in this country. Now what have we got to show for ourselves? The goddamn Cordoba." He takes another swallow of beer, his throat working like gears. "Those are some cute little girls, whose are they?"

"Mine," Cornelius whispers.

I put the can to my mouth and that first sip is like birds singing and naked women dancing and chocolate chip ice cream all at the same time.

Bud puts his briefcase on his knees, opens it up and takes out a little leather book with pictures in it. He starts showing us all kinds of pictures, tells us about his daughter, whose name is Diane and is in college and a son, Terry, who's going to high school. There's a lot of pictures and he makes sure we look at every one. There's barbecues, boat trips, beaches, kids hitting each other with plastic bats. He's even got pictures of a curly little white dog named Ace. In some of the pictures Ace is wearing a sweater.

Cornelius, even though he's trying to be Mr. Hardass, starts studying the pictures. Somebody hands over their whole life to you and you got to be a little curious.

Bud keeps on talking, going on so fast I can't keep up with it, Terry this and Diane that. He tells us about his job and his mother who's in a place for crazy people. Me and Cornelius are having a pretty good time sipping our beers and looking at the pictures, some of them are funny, seems like every picture somebody's eating or got food in their mouths. I never seen so much food. Bud shows us a picture of Disneyland and tells us a pretty good one about how his boy threw up Fritos on a movie star's shoes. He gets Cornelius laughing pretty good and then he just stops talking altogether, sits there staring at the pictures, his eyes not really seeing anything at all. We're all quiet and the sun is already down and shadows have taken over the ground and pretty soon Bud starts weeping, not loud boo-hooing, just hissing through his teeth, his big body shaking, doing his best to hold it in. He's got his eyes squeezed shut and he's shaking so hard it sounds like the chair might come apart. We wait for him to finish and finally he makes a long sigh and tilts his head back and smiles. "Boy, okay, sorry about that," he says.

He takes a few more breaths and holds out one of the pictures, points to a woman with her hair swirled and piled on top of her head, and says, "My wife, Lou Anne. Been just over four months now. Cancer that got her. Started in her stomach, you know, pretty much hollowed her out until she didn't have anything left inside. She kept plugging away a year more than the doctors gave her. She wanted to see one of her grandkids born, bless her heart. Never did make it."

He opens another pocket in his briefcase and there are more pictures, different shapes and sizes, some black and white, all of his wife. He shuffles through them, like cards, but doesn't hand them around to us. Bud hiccups a couple times, but doesn't say nothing else. I look over at Cornelius and his face has gone pale and he's grabbing his chair, the muscles in his arm standing out. He looks like he just woke up and doesn't know exactly where he's at. It's the way he used to look all the time right after Ada died. He's been getting better, but around the last new year Cornelius bought a gun off somebody, a little pistol, kept it under his mattress. One night I got up to piss and he was in the front room, holding that gun like it was something special to him, looking it down the barrel, pulling the hammer back, that kind of thing. Cornelius was concentrating so hard he didn't notice me looking in on him. Next morning while he was at work I found the gun, walked a good mile and half up the sandwash, cussing the whole way, and dropped the gun down an old mine shaft. Didn't hear it hit the bottom.

Only thing I try telling Cornelius is we got to keep going. Survive, you know. It's what we been doing for hundreds of years now.

We sit there quiet for a long time, me, Bud and my boy Cornelius. The dark is moving in from the hills, and I think about Opal, my own wife, who died having Cornelius. She put him into the world and was gone just like that, before I knew there was something wrong. And here we are now, three men sitting on a porch, three men with three dead wives.

Oh, it's a sad fucking world.

Finally Bud starts putting the pictures away, wiping his eyes, saying I'm sorry, I'm sorry, I'm a holy goddamn wreck. The girls are up on the porch now, looking at us with these big wide eyes. They know something's not right. They start to go inside and I tell them there is a snake in there and I better get it before we go inside to eat.

"Snake?" Bud says. "You got a snake in there?" His voice is still all thick and wrong.

"Sometimes they get in there, going after mice," I tell him.

I start to get up, but Bud stops me, tells me not to bother, if it's all right with me he'll find that snake and take care of it. He says it's the least he can do. "I've killed a few snakes in my time," he says. "The home is no place for a snake."

Cornelius gets up too, and tries telling Bud don't worry, that it's his house and he's going to be the one to kill the snake. All the sudden they're falling all over each other to get into the house, like nothing on this earth will keep them out of there.

They go inside and the light comes on. I can hear them clomping around, looking under things, throwing things, and then Bud yells, "Holy Shit! Watch out!" and then they're both shouting, get out of the way, grab that broom, it's going into the bathroom, look at the size of that motherfucker. They're yelling so loud because they're both scared shitless.

I don't get up to help or even to have a look, just stay in my chair with my arms around the girls. They look up at me, their eyes round as dimes. We hear Bud and Cornelius go into the bathroom and then the real commotion starts, the shouting and smashing and crashing. We hear glass breaking and all kinds of thumps and whacks and grunting and it sounds more like they're beating a mule to death in there instead of a poor old snake. It goes on for a long time, too long, the grunting and the *thong thong thong* the bathtub makes when somebody hits it. Finally it's quiet and the girls push their noses into my chest.

We sit there waiting, no sound at all, and pretty soon here comes the screen door flying open and they come out onto the porch, blood smeared on their arms. Damn, they made hamburger out of that snake. They're both holding onto it, kind of doing a little tug of war with it, their eyes all lit up and crazy. Makes me a little sorry I even mentioned the snake to anybody. The snake is so tore up and bloody I can't tell what kind it is, it's just a big long dead snake, all smashed to hell. Can't even tell which end's the head or the tail. It's about as beat-up and dead as a thing could be but it's still twitching and curling around itself. Bud finally lets go of the snake and drops the bloody coal shovel he's holding in his other hand. He bends over, panting worse than ever. I put my hand on his side to keep him steady. "We got him," he says, shaking his head and gulping air. "We showed him, by God."

Cornelius goes down the porch steps and starts walking out into the brush, dragging the snake behind him. I tell Bud that Cornelius lost his wife awhile back, too, and Bud looks up at me, his eyes wet and sad now, and he nods. Then he picks up Peaches like she's nothing but a Barbie doll, holds her up in front of him and gives her a kiss on the cheek. He does the same with Charlotte and the girls stand next to me rubbing the kisses from their faces with Bud's bloody handprints on their sleeves.

We turn back to look at Cornelius and he's dragging that snake behind him, leaning forward, like it's the heaviest thing in the world. He keeps going until he's halfway to the road and he stays there in sagebrush for a minute, staring out at nothing. Then he grabs the snake by two hands and begins twirling around, two, three times and lets it go with a loud groan. We can see the snake go spinning out into the sky like it's flying through the stars and then it lands, a little thud we can barely hear, way out in the dark.

Beautiful Places

————————————o————————————

Me and Green are heading through Utah, mountains all
around us, swinging with the Stones and milking our
ninety-dollar Monte Carlo for everything she's worth when
there's a grinding chatter and we coast to a stop knowing that
the old boat has pumped her last piston. According to the road
sign we just passed, we're on the outskirts of a place called
Logan. Me and Green look at each other and without saying
anything, come to an agreement. We got a lot more than ninety dollars' worth out of this car so we push it into a ditch at the
side of the road and start walking.

We've come all the way from Alaska where we worked on
a fishing boat for the summer. In the winter months, when all
we had was money and lots of time to spend it, we lived high

on the hog; we had salmon and moose steak daily, we drank expensive beer and gambled a lot. It would have been paradise except for the unfortunate lack of women.

When the money ran out, one of our poker buddies gave us a tip about construction jobs in Arizona. The prospect of spending another summer knee-deep in fish guts had sobered us up considerably. Not to mention the women problem. If we were sure of anything, it was that Arizona had its fair share of women. So we bought the car and headed south. We passed through Canada in spring. I don't believe I've ever seen such beauty. Some days, the sky was so blue it brought me close to tears. Imagine it: the old car humming beneath your feet, the wind like a woman's fingers in your hair, bearing the smell of pine and fresh water and mint.

Sometimes playing the Stones felt like a desecration.

About halfway through Idaho I could tell there was something wrong with Green. Green is short and skinny and is missing his right hand. He has long brown hair and a sparse, stringy affair he calls a beard. He sat there for over an hour reading the nutritional information on the back of his Coors. Green doesn't say much to start with, but he hadn't said a thing the whole day. I asked him if he planned on drinking that beer and he looked up at me, wide-eyed and startled, the kind of look my crazy Grandma Lou used to have when we'd catch her on the front lawn in the middle of the night square dancing solo in nothing but her saddle shoes.

He thought about it for awhile and then told me flat out that he didn't want to go through Utah. I said, What, and go through Nevada? Out of the question, I told him. Utah is a place of beauty. It is pure. Nevada has Las Vegas in it.

Green mumbled something to the effect that he didn't believe in beauty. That set me back some. Green is one of those dark serious types, but once in a while he'll smile and it will make your whole day. Even though I am thoroughly un-educated and only twenty-nine, I know a thing or two about beauty and I, for one, believe in it. I have seen trees full of eagles in Oregon and Sioux children riding bicycles over snowy roads in the Black Hills. I have traveled all over and have seen a good deal of the loveliest things on earth. I told Green about the things I have seen. I asked him if these things don't count as beauty.

Green went back to reading his beer and said he couldn't tell you.

It was too late to take a detour around Utah and as we entered the state I felt justified. We were in a little valley with a river to one side of us and purple mountain majesty all around. There was still snow on the peaks and in the shadowy places, and I let go of the steering wheel and held out my arms wide as if to say, Look what we might have missed!

Green paid me no attention and this was when our car gave out on us. I don't know if Green had some kind of premoni-tion about something like this happening and this is why he didn't want to go through Utah. I wouldn't doubt it. Green is a lot smarter than most people would give him credit for. You see a guy with long hair and a beard and missing his right hand and you think he's a criminal or an idiot. It's just the way people are.

We walk toward the center of town and the place seems fairly deserted. There's nobody on the streets and a car passes every once in awhile. I wonder if we have taken a real back road. When I travel, I don't use a map. I don't know how to fold the damn things, much less read them. This gets me into trouble once in awhile, but I adjust. Sometimes I'll end up in a town that doesn't even have a gas station or maybe I'll find myself on a road that leads to nowhere, just stops dead at a wheat field or gradually gets narrower and full of weeds until there isn't a road anymore. I'll take surprises like this over maps any day.

We're walking along and I ask Green what his theory might be as to why there's nobody around. The road is wide and new and right now we are passing a shopping center. I don't figure he'll give me an answer; Green is mad at me for coming into Utah. When Green is mad he generally doesn't say anything at all. We walk along for quite a stretch and Green says, It's Sunday. I don't know if this is an answer to my question or just a comment on things, but I don't push it, I'm just glad Green is speaking.

After we've walked a mile or so we hear singing, singing so beautiful it could break your heart or make you sterile. We have no choice but to walk to it. Green doesn't seem to be so keen about going toward the singing but he follows me anyway. The music is coming from a big gray church on a hill. The church's tall doors are opened wide and it's like angels singing in heaven. I stand there and let it float around me, my eyes closed until it stops. At times like this I wonder why I'm not a religious man.

Me and Green are down to pocket change, and I, for one, am hungry. We spent our last twenty-dollar bill for gas in Idaho Falls. Stairs lead up to the doors and I go stand at the bottom of them. I figure that if you ever need a hand, a church can't be a bad place to start. Green lets me know that no offense against God, but he'd rather not go into that church. I tell him if anyone is going into the church, it will be me. I climb the stairs and inside the doors is some kind of entrance room with people sitting on padded benches. They all stare at me and I act like I'm admiring the architecture. There are a couple of women holding crying babies and a few other young folks all done up in ties and dresses. In the main room, which I can't see, someone is talking about the final days. One of those babies is screeching like the world is coming to an end this very second.

I notice a kid with a crewcut who doesn't seem to be enjoying himself. He's fidgeting and he has the look of someone who has just swallowed something unpleasant. I catch his eye and motion for him to come out. He's about nineteen or twenty and big-boned. He looks around and steps outside but keeps his distance. I hold out my hand. He shakes it and retreats a few feet.

I tell him my name and explain to him our situation: coming from Alaska, our car breaking down, no money or food. I ask the kid if he knows where we could find a bit of work so we can make enough money to buy a bus ticket to Arizona or at least get some lunch.

The kid looks at me, perplexed. I feel bad for getting him out of church and taking advantage of the Christian charity that has most likely been so recently drilled into him.

Maybe you know someone who needs their lawn mowed, I say.

The kid looks back into the church and then around at the houses on the street. He says, I don't think you can find much work, it being Sunday.

He looks down at Green who has his hands in his pockets, trying to hide the one that's not there. Green is watching water go down the gutter.

We don't want handouts, I say, which is the truth.

You could mow my lawn if I had one, the kid says. Maybe you want to wash my car? I have a car.

We wash cars, I say. We're experts.

Good deal, he says.

Just trying to break the ice a little, I point to the kid's hair and say, That's quite a hairdo you've got. When I was in the army they made us cut our hair like that. What's your excuse?

The kid stares at me. I was expecting at least a smile but I'm not getting one. After a minute I say, Why don't we go get that car washed?

We go down the stairs and get Green and the kid acquainted, whose name we find out is Wade. He's got ears like Frisbees and nice teeth. He wears a tie and cowboy boots. I've never seen anybody do that before.

We get in his car and he takes us to his apartment. Wade has a garter belt hanging from his rearview mirror and if the tapes on the floor are any clue, listens to an almost unhealthy amount of heavy metal. I wonder what a guy like this would be doing in church.

Where are you guys from? Wade says.

I tell him I'm originally from Pittsburgh, and even though I haven't been back in a number of years I am still a dyed-in-the-wool Steelers fan and follow the Pirates when I can.

What about you? Wade says to Green.

Green says, I am from nowhere, really. All over, I guess. I myself don't know where Green is from. I don't even know how he lost his hand. Green has said to me that he doesn't talk about things that have happened in the past because they're over with and why talk about them? Back in Alaska I would get him really drunk and once in awhile he would talk about the old days. I never got him to say anything about how he lost his hand but once he told me about the wife he used to have, and the two kids, and how they went to a zoo and a tiger peed all over them from about twenty feet away. We laughed about that until we peed all over ourselves. After we got cleaned up, Green kept telling me about his wife and kids. It was like once he started he couldn't stop. He told me about the trips they took and how he taught his two boys to play chess before they turned five. They were geniuses, he said. Einsteins.

I don't think Green remembers telling me all this. At least he's never mentioned it. Someday I plan to ask him to tell me where his family is, what happened to them. I think this would explain some things. Someday, when we've been together long enough for Green to trust me, he will tell me everything. I don't doubt it a bit.

So we wash and wax Wade's car with some stuff he gave us. The car is an old Cougar, painted gold, with mags and a spoiler—the works. We labor over that car with a sense of pleasure. It has been so long since I washed a car that it feels more like entertainment than a chore.

Green seems to have loosened up, and that helps. He even whistles while he buffs the hood with a rag that's twisted around the stump of his wrist. I spray Armor All on the tires and wipe the chrome so clean I can see the pores on my face in it. I try to keep my mind on my work but girls in long dresses walk by and I am instantly distracted. When a breeze blows their skirts about their calves I feel something flutter down the length of my spine. Green doesn't even notice them.

When we're done, the car is a bright and sparkling wonder, a revelation.

I say to Green, This is beauty, right before your very face and we are responsible for it.

Green doesn't say anything, but he smiles and even though we're stuck in some place without a car or money and have to wash some kid's car just so we can eat, we are truly happy about it.

Wade comes out with a sack of food in his arms. He's got some faded Wranglers on and he now looks a natural in boots. He's got a dog with him, a blue and black-spotted cow dog with two different colors of eyes: green and yellow. The dog's narrow face and eyes make it look intelligent somehow. It looks smarter than the majority of my friends.

Wade says, You guys are professionals.

I just make a humble shrug and say, Shucks. Green rubs the dog's ears.

Wade says, I'd invite you guys in for lunch, but I've got too many roommates in there taking up space. I know a place we can go to eat without a lot of noise.

He takes us to a nice shady spot next to the river, says this is where he likes to take his girlfriends when privacy is needed. It is getting to be late in the day and there seem to be blackbirds everywhere, squawking and flapping in the trees. Robert (the dog's name, as Wade has informed us) scrambles out of the car and makes a beeline for the river. He jumps in with a huge splash and paddles around, yapping like crazy.

Dog's a fish, Wade says, shaking his head.

We sit down under a cottonwood and eat ham sandwiches and huge amounts of store-bought macaroni salad. We watch the dog and laugh. He's on the other side of the river, sopping wet and jumping high in the air to snap at buzzing june bugs.

We're finishing off the last box of Ding Dongs when Wade says to Green, What happened to your hand?

I watch Green pick at the grass and I hold my breath. Nobody, including me, has ever asked that question point-blank. Still tearing up grass, he says in a low voice, Got smashed in some machinery where I worked down in St. George. They had to take it off.

Wade says, So you're from down south.

Green just nods. I don't know what to say, so I keep my mouth shut. Green looks up at Wade.

You a Mormon? he says. You were in that church.

Wade nods, says, Try to be. You?

I was for a while, Green says. My wife wanted me to be one

so they baptized me. I was the Scout leader for a couple of years.

Green has a funny look on his face, a look I've never seen before. His eyebrows are pushed up and together. He looks desperate. I continue to keep my mouth shut.

I was a Scout, Wade says. Almost an Eagle but I took cigarettes to a camp-out once and they never let me back.

Green sighs and says, They'll do that.

Wade puts the last Ding Dong in his mouth. It looks like a hockey puck. Robert comes back to us and lies down next to Wade, munching on a june bug and smelling like a wet dog. The sun is right on us now, just above the mountains and coming in through the leaves. The top of Wade's crew cut shines and Green's face is hidden in the shadow of his own hair.

I still know a few hymns, Green says. I always liked the hymns.

He whistles part of a nice song I've heard him whistle before.

I just don't know the words, he says.

I can't sing, Wade says. Never could.

Wade says to me, You a Mormon, too?

Nope, I say. Though I wish I was one at the moment, for some reason. To tell the truth I don't know exactly what a Mormon is. Somebody says Mormon and I think of old men in beards and black hats. This Wade is a Mormon. Green says he used to be. I would never have guessed Green was a one-time churchgoer. All of this is definitely interesting.

I listen to them while they swap a few Boy Scout stories and talk about Wade's problem with everybody wanting him to be a missionary. I have never heard Green talk so much and I'm fairly certain he's not drunk. He even gives Wade some advice about women.

I listen for as long as I can, but there is something so tight in my chest it almost hurts and I can't listen anymore. I get up and throw off my clothes and jump with Robert into the river. The water is cold and deep; it comes from old glaciers close to the sky. The current is slow and pushes me slowly forward and down. Robert and me chase each other back and forth. I look over from time to time where Green and Wade are talking and laughing. They are discussing religious matters while I'm in the river with a dog.

After a while Green and Wade strip down to their underwear and dive in after us. Green's skin is so white it is almost blue. Wade comes up, water rolling off him, sputtering like a kid. He takes Green in a bear hug and dunks him under. I whoop like a drunk Italian and jump on both of them. Robert gets ahold of my arm with his teeth and tries to pull me away. The water is so cold we all have to yell. Even Robert howls.

The sun is on the water in pieces, and blackbirds and june bugs zoom around our heads. Once we're all in the river, gulping water and splashing around, I just don't care that Green opened up to this kid he's known less than a day after staying closed with me for so long. Green is free and easy, the happiest I've seen him for a long time and I can't help but be happy too. I get him in a headlock and we wrestle like alligators.

The current pushes at our legs, dragging us slowly along to where the sun in going down. We stop struggling and let it take us; we let everything go in that river. I close my eyes and I am so numb it's like I am floating on air toward some place full of light and quiet. I get out only when the pain between my legs reminds me what all this cold might do to the general health of my gonads.

I struggle up on the bank and see that the current has taken me farther than the others. Green is already under the tree trying to get his clothes on and not having much luck. When you're one-handed and shivering to beat the band, putting on your clothes can be a pretty awkward process. I run over and help him get his legs in his pants.

Once we get his shirt buttoned up Green says, We should be on our way. It's almost dark.

The peaceful look he had in the river is gone. Now he is back to his pinched, worried self. His hair is sopping wet and he looks like he's just had the water squeezed out of him.

We need to get going if we're ever going to make those construction jobs, he says. We can hitchhike if we have to.

Wade comes up from the river, tiptoeing among the weeds and sharp rocks with Robert right behind him. The cold water has turned Wade a bright pink. He is rubbing himself and saying, Oh mama, oh mama.

I stand there, a light breeze raising goose bumps all over me and say, This would be my only wish right now: a big fluffy towel, a hot bubble bath and massage afterwards, preferably at the hands of a female.

You guys are welcome to my apartment, Wade says. I can supply at least some of that. And I have a sleeping bag and some blankets. We'll get some tickets and I'll take you to the bus station in the morning. I look at Green who is putting our garbage into a paper sack. I don't understand it, but I can tell that his only wish right now is to get out of here as quick as possible. He looks like he's ready to bolt any second.

I think for a minute and say, Thanks a million, but we've got to keep moving. These construction jobs won't wait forever.

Putting on his clothes, Wade says, Then let me take you to the bus station now. I'll get the tickets. You did a hell of a job on my car.

You took us out here and gave us lunch, Green says, his face twisted and unreadable. You've been too nice already. If you can just drop us off some place we can get a ride.

Wade rubs his hand over his damp head and looks confused. I feel pretty much the same way. Not being the pushy type, Wade just shrugs a little and takes us to the other end of town where the main street turns into the highway that will take us to Salt Lake. He gives us forty dollars and tells us it's the money for our car.

He says, tomorrow I'll tow it over to the junk yard. LeRoy Dooley is a friend of my father. He'll give me at least that much for it.

For some reason I want to give Wade a hug but I wouldn't know how to go about it so instead I deliver the most sincere handshake possible. Green gives him a nervous handshake, thanking him for everything, and turns away. We both give Robert a scratch between the ears before Wade drives back into Logan.

We get a ride with an old couple as far as Salt Lake and just before dawn we get on with a trucker headed for Phoenix. Once we're in the cab, the road moving away beneath us and the musty old guy next to us telling bad jokes one after the other, Green finally settles down a little. The wrinkles in his forehead smooth away and he puts his head against the window and closes his eyes. The light is just coming up, turning the snow on the mountains purple and orange. The sky is opening sharp and clear. I can't be sure, but I think a place like this is just a little too beautiful for Green to stand.

He Becomes Deeply and Famously Drunk

———————————————o———————————————

I am a cowboy. There are others in this outfit who prefer to call themselves ranch hands or just "hands," maybe they think *cowboy* is a little too flamboyant for this day and age, who knows, but shit, I herd cows, I vaccinate, brand, dehorn and castrate cows, more often than not I smell exactly like a cow—I am a cowboy. I've been at this for nine months now and I figure I've earned the right to call myself whatever in God's name I please.

I am two months shy of eighteen years old, I'm covered with freckles and am quite good-looking if I can believe what the girls tell me. I am also a natural loudmouth which has caused me no end of grief and misery. Pretty much all my life I've been hearing the same thing: take it easy, Archie, put a lid on it Archie, pipe the hell down. You hear this enough it gets on your nerves.

One of the good things about this kind of work: I can really let loose, talking and shouting and singing—at the top of my lungs if I want to and out in the brush there's no one to give a hooey but the cows. Something about my voice scares the cows, some of them are terrified of me, I swear it, when they hear me they get this rolling wild look in their eyes and start to running and climbing all over each other. My horse, Loaf, gets annoyed by all my talking and singing and every once in awhile she'll reach back and bite the hell out of my leg. I don't mind, I just hit her back, a good sock on the side of the head, and she won't try anything like that again for at least a couple weeks.

Before I came to work here I had this idea that A & C Ranch would be this big beautiful spread, full of rivers and green rolling hills, like that TV show *Big Valley*. I imagined myself as Heath Barkley, riding around on a shiny roan, wearing a vest and a silk scarf, smoking a long cigarillo and shooting bad guys lurking in the bushes. The actual ranch, I was sorry to learn, is plain and relatively small: fifteen hundred acres of overgrazed scrub land that can't support more than two hundred head at any one time. Mr. Platt, who is richer and more of a recluse than God, has his thousand-head herd spread out all over the place, on at least fourteen other pieces of land between here and the Navajo reservation, most of it government-owned. The sad truth is we spend more time zipping around in our pickup trucks than we do on our good and noble horses.

Today, for instance, we've got to go up around Sell's Pasture, a good forty-five-minute drive, to fix a busted windmill, a rickety fifty-footer that is a horror to climb. Of course it will be me, the new guy, climbing to the top of the damn thing, risking my neck and reputation. It's about five in the morning and I'm in the shower, singing the jingles to every TV commercial I can think of. Richard bangs on the bathroom door and shouts, "Archie, keep it down in there! Got-damn!"

This is exactly what I'm talking about. I can't even take a shower without somebody having an opinion about it. Richard is one of the hands, he and I share a trailer out here on the ranch. He is the oldest of us, the veteran, and apparently his job is to keep an eye on me. Richard is short and middle-aged and one of these days I'm going to pick up his scrawny little body and break it over my knee if he is not careful. This morning Richard woke me up at five a.m. the way he does every morning, by shouting right in my ear, *Come to, you candy corn son of a bitch!* He learned this particular wake-up call in the Army and inflicts it on me each and every day. This kind of thing makes Richard feel like the big enchilada, so I let him get away with it.

I yodel about six more jingles and then towel off and walk into the kitchen for a piece of toast, and Ted, the foreman, is there explaining to Richard how he wants to do things today. Ted lives in the old ranch house up on the hill with his wife and little girl. He had some serious childhood ailment and now he's got a lumpy oversized head and hearing aids strapped to his big loose ears.

"Change of plans," Ted says to me. "I'm taking Richard with me to help bring in the heifers from Copper Springs. I want you to pick up Jesus and get that windmill fixed. Take your time and fix it right. Take all day if you have to."

"And put some pants on," Richard says. Richard absolutely hates my guts because I am bigger, younger, handsomer, and a hell of a lot smarter than he is.

I lift up the towel and show him my bare butt: one of the attributes women enjoy most about me. I sing a line from

"Moon Over Georgia" in a girlish falsetto and do a few soft-shoe shuffles on the kitchen linoleum.

Richard just sits there, red-faced, shoveling plain oatmeal into his mouth, unable to come up with anything to say. He is one of these literal types who simply cannot comprehend sarcasm or humor of any sort. He reaches over and grabs the Volume A encyclopedia from the kitchen counter and begins studying it, his nose inches from the page. About six months ago Richard decided that he was going to get himself educated. Instead of wasting all that time and money on a college education, he decided to read the entire Encyclopedia Brittanica, the whole blasted thing, from A to Z.

Richard is terribly proud of himself for coming up with a way to become a genius and a scholar for only $99.95 in twelve easy monthly installments. Problem is, it's been over half a year now and Richard is only about a third of the way through the first volume. He is now an authority on aardvarks, acupuncture, and John Adams, but he'll be collecting social security before he could tell you what a zygote is.

I go back to the laundry room and take Doug off his perch. He acts happy to see me, bobs his head and hunches his shoulders. I get a piece of dog kibble from a bag in the cupboard and he snatches it out of my hand so quick you'd think he's dying of starvation.

Doug is an eight year-old male turkey vulture. Because he doesn't get much exercise, he's a little overweight, but he is a good bird, and I've become attached to him; some nights when he has trouble sleeping, I'll take him to bed with me and hold him against my chest until he gets drowsy enough to go to sleep perched on my bedpost. He used to belong to one R. L. Ledbetter, who worked for Mr. Platt and lived in this trailer with Richard until one early morning a couple of years ago when R.L. got run over by a garbage truck crossing the road. R.L. had worked for a few years as a rodeo clown and used Doug (short for Douglas Fairbanks) in one of his acts. In this rodeo act, R.L. would act like he got shot by a villain, and Doug would come flying in out of nowhere, land on his chest and start picking at him. R.L. trained Doug to do this by hiding a Corn Nut somewhere on his person and Doug would go picking around until he found it, R.L. squirming and cringing whenever Doug got too near his crotch. Apparently rodeo crowds found this hilarious.

Even though Richard doesn't enjoy Doug's company all that much, he is convinced he can teach Doug to talk. Sometimes I'll come home and find Richard at the kitchen table, with Doug perched on the back of a chair and Richard saying something like, "Come on, Doug, say 'bazooka.' Ba-*zoo*-ka." And Doug sitting there mum as a fence post, watching barn swallows buzzing past the window. Richard says he read somewhere that vultures have the same vocal apparatus as parrots, and with enough persistence he thinks Doug could become a talking vulture. So far, Doug hasn't said a word.

I go back into my room where I put on jeans, a T-shirt—it's going to be a hot son of a bitch out there today—and a pair of workboots. I have to wear these run-of-the-mill clodhoppers because I've yet to find a pair of cowboy boots that will fit my splayed feet. When I go outside and fire up the old Ford the sun is just coming up and long shadows stretch out under the sage and creosote. I let the engine run for a minute, then I lay on the accelerator like Richard Petty in his prime, spraying dust and gravel everywhere, and head out on Witchicume Road, on my way to pick up Jesus.

I came out to the A & C to get my life turned around. My mother made the arrangements, did all the sweet-talking to get me out here and her theory goes something like this: you take your loudmouth juvenile delinquent with bad table manners, stick him out in the middle of nowhere, bust his balls with honest hard labor, and maybe, just maybe, he will turn out to be the upstanding citizen you hoped for all along. I'm pretty certain the folks out here weren't all that hot to hire a city kid with no ranch experience and a history with the law, but Ted was an old acquaintance of my father, and finally he gave in.

The truth is I've always wanted to come back, always harbored secret desires about strapping on the chaps and riding fences. I was born only forty miles from here, in Holbrook, and I lived on the ranch the first four and a half years of my life until my father was killed and my mother took me to live in Stillwater, Oklahoma, her hometown. My father was the ranch foreman and we lived in the old house where Ted and his family live now. Even though I can't remember anything at all about living here, I did some work on this ranch, in my own way, all those years ago. My mother told me that the winter I turned four, my father would take me out on the feed runs, put the old International into compound and let me steer, kneeling on the seat, while he stood in the back, breaking bales and pitching hay to the cows standing in the snow.

In Oklahoma I spent my energy talking too much, getting into fights, drinking booze, smashing mailboxes, pretty much being obnoxious however and wherever I could. I have something wrong with me, something bad inside that builds up until I have to let it out by talking, shouting, raging, letting it all loose, even if there is no one there to listen. (I even thrash and holler in my sleep sometimes—one more thing Richard holds against me.) But there are times when the only way I can get back to feeling normal again is by beating the shit out of someone who may not even deserve it, or by destroying something, it doesn't really matter what. When I feel this way, I get to punching or smashing or kicking and I can feel this blackness pouring out of me and I just keep going, it's a great feeling, just letting go, flailing away, until I feel empty and clean again. I've hurt some people and wrecked a lot of perfectly innocent cars, dishware, phone booths, electronic goods, what have you. Even though a lot of my teachers called me gifted (over and over again: unlimited potential! a diamond in the rough!), I never finished high school because they finally kicked me out once and for all. I've been arrested for battery, disorderly conduct, theft, vandalism, disturbing the peace, assaulting a police officer. I've been on probation since I was eleven years old.

I've seen therapists, psychiatrists, clergymen, even a hypnotist. My mother had high hopes for the hypnotist, but for some reason in my second session with the poor old guy I came out of my trance and sucker-punched him a good one right in the face. I don't remember doing it, only remember waking up and seeing him sitting on the carpet, his nose spattered on his face like a piece of rotten watermelon.

I have a probation officer, Ms. Condley, who calls Ted every week to make sure I haven't busted anyone's lip or committed an act of debauchery. Ms. Condley calls me every week, too, and asks me about my feelings, about my dreams and aspirations, it's all very sensitive, but she never says goodbye without reminding me that if I break my probation, if I slip up even a little, get even a little drunk or involve myself in some minor fisticuffs, I'll be sent off to boot camp and won't get out till I'm twenty-nine. So far I have been able to keep my ass clean. My only serious difficulty is keeping myself from beating the daylights out of Richard.

A few weeks before I moved back out here I went to the public library and stole the only book I could find on cowboys. I wanted to get some general how-to information (how to put on a saddle, how to make a lasso, how to mount a horse) so that when I got here I wouldn't look like a complete fool. The book didn't give tips or anything like that, it was just a lot of quaint old bullshit about the cowboys of yore. I read the whole thing anyway. Under a pen and ink drawing of a couple of dirty cowpunchers weaving down Main Street, arm in arm, clutching half-empty whiskey bottles, was this caption:

After a mythic cattle drive or a bone-wearying spring roundup, the cowboy, looking for release and diversion, commonly finds his way to the nearest saloon where he becomes deeply and famously drunk.

I remember this because it describes to a T my father and the way he died. Like the cowboys in the picture, he liked to celebrate after a big job by getting himself good and hammered. It was his only vice and the one thing my mother could not stand about him. The day he died, they had finished getting the herd down off the mountain for the winter (nearly a two-week job) and he went into town to throw a few down with his crew at the Sure Seldom. He was two solid hours into his drinking when Calfred Pulsipher, a piece-of-shit well-digger with a lazy eyeball, came around to pick a fight. Calfred and my father had been good friends in their younger years, but Calfred had carried a grudge against my father ever since he lost his starting quarterback job to him on the Salado Wildcats eight-man football team. Apparently, Calfred said some terrible things about my mother, right there in front of my father's crew—sick, perverted things— and finally my father invited Calfred outside to settle it. Calfred went outside first and in the thirty seconds or so it took my drunk father to find the door, Calfred had time to pick up an industrial jack from the back of his pickup. When my father stepped out into the cold night air, ready to whip

Calfred's sorry ass and be done with it, Calfred brought down the jack full force, right on top of his head. My father went down, stayed face down in the gravel for a minute or so, dead still, and suddenly got up punching with everything he had, as if the blow not only sobered him up but also lit a fire under his ass. He got some fine licks in on Calfred before one of the sheriff's deputies came and arrested them both.

Even though my father's head had stopped bleeding, the sheriff wanted to call the ambulance in from Round Valley (there was no doctor in Salado in those days) but my father kept assuring everyone he was feeling fine, all he needed was a few more drinks to get rid of the headache he was having. In the end, the sheriff stuck them both in the same jail cell to sleep off their drunk. Some time that night in that puke-smelling cell full of drunks and no-goods and bums, my father died of bleeding in the brain, his head resting on the lap of Calfred Pulsipher, the man who killed him.

Out here in Arizona, Jesus is my only real friend. He is a tiny wetback, barely five feet tall with his boots on and even though he's lived on American soil for over two decades his English is as piss-poor as if he showed up here last Christmas. He has star-quality teeth and likes to keep his hair coifed and oiled with one curl hanging down on his forehead in the manner of old time movie actors. He's worked for Mr. Platt off and on for a good many years and while the others here resented me, pissed on me for being young and ignorant, enjoyed watching me make a fool of myself, Jesus helped me out from the start, taking time to show how to dally a rope, say, or throw a calf for branding.

Right now Jesus is explaining, in his own way, why he doesn't like people calling him a Mexican. He doesn't consider himself a Mexican at all, he says, because he is actually a full-blooded Yaqui Indian and very proud of it, a direct descendant of the Aztecs, who were, according to him, the most proud and powerful nation the world ever saw. And who, according to him, had it not been for malaria, typhoid and other white-man plagues, would have kicked some Spaniard ass.

"I'm not eh-Spanish," he says, thumping his chest like a little brown Tarzan. "I'm Yaqui."

"It's not *eh*-Spanish," I say. "That's not how you say it. You got to get your S's right. She sells seashells by the sea shore. Okay, I'm going to say a word and you repeat. Snoopy."

"Eh-Snoopy," Jesus says.

"Sssssnoopy," I say.

"Ehhhhh-snoopy," Jesus says.

"Ah shit," I say.

"Ah shit," says Jesus, proud of himself for making such great advancement in the language.

The guy truly is hopeless. Since he has done so much for me, I figured the least I could do was help him polish his English, but now, after nine months of correcting his pronunciation and word order, he hasn't improved a bit.

"Why don't you want to be an American?" I say. "All you have to do is get your green card, you've lived here long enough. Then you won't have to run from the border patrol any more."

"American?" Jesus says, a look of disgust twisting his wide brown face. "Americanos fat pigs, you know, honk honk."

"I'm fat, is that what you're saying?"

Jesus lifts up my T-shirt to have a look. He nods gravely. "Maybe," he says.

We stop for gas and coffee at Sud Baker's, a little eatery/truck stop. Once we've finished off our eggs and sausage, and with Jesus taking forever in the john, I pick up a loose copy of the local paper, *The Apache County Sentinel*, and there, right on the front page is that son of a bitch Calfred Pulsipher himself. It looks like an old wedding picture: Calfred's got these ridiculous lambchop sideburns and a thick polyester tie and one of his eyes, his left one, seems to be looking at the mole on his forehead while the other is pointed straight ahead. A fat woman, Calfred's wife, I guess, is sitting next to him, all dressed up. Underneath the picture it reads, *The Pulsipher children would like to congratulate Calfred and Erma on the occasion of their twenty-fifth wedding anniversary.*

A trembling starts in my stomach and moves out to my arms and hands. When I first got here I tried to look up Calfred's name in the phone book and when I couldn't find it, I convinced myself that he was dead or had moved away to Alaska. I thought I wouldn't have to worry about him anymore.

A secret: since I was five years old I have been a murderer in my heart. I've tortured, mutilated, torn, skewered, beaten, killed Calfred Pulsipher ten thousand times over. I've burned his house down, kidnapped his children, cut the head off his dog. I've dreamed, time and again, about being there that night at the Sure Seldom. In my dreams I've stopped him from killing my father in various ways, perforating him with an ice pick, shotgunning him in the gut, beating him bloody with a chain. I even made plans, back when I was twelve or thirteen and crazed with puberty, for stealing a car and a big-ass case of dynamite and coming all the way out here and blowing him into the outer reaches of space.

Growing up, I used to read a lot, mostly Zane Grey and Louis L'Amour, and in those books if someone killed a member of your family or a even a friend, it was pretty much your *duty* to pay the son of a bitch back. It's what anyone who had any courage or sense of justice did; it's what cowboys did. It's what my father would have done.

My father's name was Quinn. He was a big man with a barrel chest, curly red hair, a missing front tooth—everybody loved him. He lost the tooth to the back hoof of an Appaloosa gelding and he never got it fixed because he thought the hole in his face made him look friendlier. He was an excellent golfer (ten handicap), liked old blues music, and had a deep-seated fear of bees. Although I was a kid, not much more than a toddler when he died, I know all kinds of things—facts, stories, anecdotes—about him. After my mother took me away to Stillwater, friends would call or sometimes stop in and they'd tell me things my father used to do, the kind of man he was. I remember a few of the visitors, usually it would be a man in Wranglers, alone, or maybe with a frizzy-haired woman with big earrings, and always they'd say things like, *Oh my God, he looks just like Quinn, doesn't he?* Or, *Listen there, he's even got Quinn's voice.* And without fail my mother would break down and have to leave the room.

My mother, I think, went certifiably crazy during the year after my father's death. Nobody really knows about this except me, because I was the only one who got to witness all the lunatic things she did. One of my clearest memories is of my mother, just a few days after we'd moved to Stillwater, running outside in only her underwear as a stranger's car pulled up to the curb, hysterical and shouting, "I knew he'd come back, oh my God, you're back! Look Archie, Daddy's home!" Or the time she ripped through the house, clearing out cupboards and cabinets, trashing the attic, sure my father was there because she could smell his English Leather cologne.

Finally, she went to see a doctor who introduced her to the wonderful world of pills. It's a world she's been living in ever since.

Now, out here on the ranch, I'm always finding reminders
of him. A few weeks ago, I was down near the mud pond just
south of the big house, mending fence with Richard when I
found the letter Q carved deep into one of the anchor posts
near the dam. It's kind of a tradition out here for the person
that builds a fence to carve his initial into the final anchor post
and I knew without a doubt it was my father that had done it.
I imagined him there in the very spot I was standing, his shirt
off, his big round shoulders covered with sweat, making
cracks with his crew and grinning that gap-toothed grin
while he cut his first initial into the thick cedar post with a
buck knife.

By the time Jesus and I get to Sell's Pasture it is already
upwards of ninety degrees and with the white sun burning
into everything it feels like we're moving across the surface
of Venus. After we pull off the highway, I have to guide the
truck over three or four miles of a rutted two-track, me and
Jesus bouncing all over the seat, the stiff sagebrush on the
truck's underside like fingernails on a chalkboard. On our
way over to the windmill Jesus notices a bad case of pinkeye
on a Hereford calf. By the time he's got the medicine kit
from the glove compartment, run the calf down on foot, las-
soed it, thrown it to the ground and begun to doctor the eye,
all the time keeping one eye on the calf's very pissed-off
mother, I've climbed the ladder up to the platform and am
doing my best to dismantle the windmill head and see what
the problem is.

The windmill stopped working only a few days ago, so the
galvanized holding tank is still half full of algae-green water
and a few mangy cows are hanging around to check out
what's going on. They don't have anything better to do, blink-
ing those big dull eyes. I'll tell you one thing about cows:

they're dumb-asses. They're so dumb it's hard to understand how stupid they really are.

Once in awhile I'll look down and see a metallic flash in the green water—huge shaggy goldfish and carp they put in the tanks to keep the algae down. These things grow to be as big as poodles and they swim around flapping their tails like they own the tank.

About a hundred yards away, over next to a juniper tree, Jesus struggles to keep the bawling calf down while performing the delicate work of injecting medicine directly into its eyeball with a syringe. I shout encouragements from up on my perch and Jesus grunts and hisses and calls the calf a big-time donkey turd. By the time he's done he's sweating, covered with dust, the calf has crapped green pudding all over his pearl-buttoned shirt and what's worse, it's not even ten o'clock in the morning. He walks up to the holding tank, slings his hat like a Frisbee, sheds the rest of his clothes and steps in, the thick water closing around him. He slides down so that his head is just above water, still as a turtle on a rock.

I am banging away with my Vise-Grips at a stuck bolt, trying to loosen it, when I miss the bolt completely. My momentum throws me off balance, the whole windmill shifting underneath me, and I slip sideways off the side of the platform. I grab one of the supports to keep myself from falling, but my legs are dangling out from under me and with my White Mule work gloves on I can't get a good grip on the smooth, two-inch pipe. My hands begin to slide and my stomach curls up on itself and I look down past my feet and try to figure out the best way to fall without snapping my spine. Below me, Jesus leaps out of the tank, naked as a newborn, the huge fish writhing and bucking in the swampy water, and begins scrambling up the metal scaffolding, his wet hands and feet causing him to slip and flail and clutch.

I start bellowing, a loud panicked sound like a heifer giving birth, which causes all the cows in sight to spook and set
off sprinting for the safety of the trees. Somehow I hold out,
yelling the whole time, until Jesus reaches the platform from
the other side and grabs my belt and with the strength of a
man twice his size hauls me up.

I lie on my back for a minute staring at the blank sky and
listening to my heart thumping so hard it sounds like bones
are popping in my chest. Above me Jesus is standing there
all goose-pimply with this huge grin on his face, as if my near-
death experience has made his day. He keeps shaking his
head; he just can't get over it. "Arshie hanging, feet kicking,
help, help!" Jesus says, pantomiming the whole incident. "Arshie
shouting like woman, oooooha!, every cow runs away."

I get up and try to grab him but he ducks out of the way and
cowers at the corner of the platform, mocking me, covering
his head with his hands. "Big fat Americano scaring me. Oh
boy," he says.

I stop going after him; I'm still a little nervous about one of
us falling off this thing, and then I notice that Jesus has the
biggest pecker I've ever seen. I get a good look at it and there's
no doubt—I've been in a lot of locker rooms and seen quite a
few, but this one takes the cake.

"That's a considerable pecker you've got there," I tell him,
keeping a good grip on one of the supports.

He looks down at it, lifts it up with his hand like it's a vegetable he's considering purchasing at the supermarket. "Oh
mama," he says.

He picks up the Vise-Grips, goes right to work on the stuck
bolt, and starts lamenting that his wife took his kids to visit
relatives down in Mexico and it's been two long weeks since
his *pendejo* saw any action. He begins to croon some mournful
Sonoran ballad, using the Vise-Grips like a microphone, and

for some reason it seems perfectly appropriate that he is nude and fifty feet in the air.

We get the head dismantled and find that the windmill needs nothing more than new suction leathers. In no time at all we've got the thing fixed, put back together, and I've joined Jesus down in the cow tank.

The inside of the tank is as slimy as frog innards and the huge fish curl around my stomach and legs and I still haven't decided whether the whole sensation is disgusting or kind of pleasant. We sit there for awhile and even though the windmill has been fixed, there is no wind to speak of and the big fan is completely still and useless as before. This kind of silence drives me crazy and I bear it for as long as I can until I ask the question I've been waiting to ask somebody for nine months: "You know who Calfred Pulsipher is?"

Jesus, who appeared to be falling asleep, sits up and looks right at me, but he only shrugs and mumbles something I can't understand.

"What?" I say.

"Nada, nada," he says.

"Do you know him?"

"Pool-see-fur," Jesus says, rolling the word across his tongue. I don't mind Jesus screwing around with me but sometimes he drives me nuts.

"Come on, you Mexican," I say. "Does he live around here?"

"Oh, he live around somewhere."

"Where?"

Now he's giving me that sly half grin that Latin males everywhere are famous for. "Why you want to know?"

Since I've been here I haven't talked about Calfred Pulsipher or my father with anyone and now that I have, it feels like I've betrayed myself in some way. Even though I'm pretty sure everybody on the ranch knows my situation, not one of them has ever mentioned it, and that's the way I like it.

We look at each other across the tank, Jesus waiting for an answer and me not ready to give it.

Finally a mangy Hereford, either a very brave or a very stupid one, comes strolling right up to the tank to have a drink. Jesus hollers at the cow, calling it some of the most vile words in the English language and his pronunciation is absolutely perfect.

I didn't believe I could actually *enjoy* ranch work. I've heard some of the hands complain about certain kinds of work, mostly jobs that require getting down out of the saddle, but I pretty much love it all: branding, clearing ditches, building fence, irrigating. I love hauling hay, throwing those bales around as if they have *offended* me. I don't even mind getting up before the crack of dawn, even if I have to do it with Richard the army general barking in my ear. I like the way the world feels empty at that time of day; it seems as if you are the only one alive, early in the morning when you're up before everybody else and you can step out into the low light with your cup of coffee and hear a horse chewing grass from two hundred yards away.

Every day you get something new thrown at you; I mean, one thing I've never been around here is bored. You work all day, so busy sweating and busting your ass that you don't even have time to think; you go and go and go until you look up and notice the sun is nearly down and it's time to pack it in. There's nothing as nice as that ride home; the truck rumbling loosey-goosey down the road with a mind of its own, the radio hissing out Mexican trumpets, that sweet aching tiredness settling deep in your joints. You go home and fix yourself some dinner and even though it's nothing more than chili out of a can and a tube of instant biscuits it's the best damned meal you've ever had.

The only thing that will ruin a day like this is getting a call from my mother. My mother calls once or twice a week to make sure I'm caught up on all her problems. A few days ago she called me just as we were getting in from a day of calving out heifers to tell me that she had broken up with her boyfriend.

"Archie?" she said. "Archie? Are you there, honey?" Her voice was as high-pitched as a train whistle.

"I'm right here," I said.

Suddenly she began to weep and I knew immediately that she had taken too many of one pill or had mixed some up that weren't supposed to be mixed. She was speaking in that hysterical little-girl voice that I remember hearing so much after my father was killed.

"He left me, Arch, he's gone." She was practically shrieking. I didn't know who the hell she was talking about. I was able to piece together that her current boyfriend, a hot tub salesman named Chet, had decided to go back to his ex-wife in Florida. I told her I was sure she'd be able to find another boyfriend in a day or two.

"I miss you honey," she cried. "I want to see you. You're the only one left."

A number of times she's called me, trying to get me to come home, even though she herself is the one that did what was necessary to get me out here. One particularly bad night a couple of months ago she accused me of abandoning her, just as my father had done. Every time I talk to her it breaks the spell; I'm not Archie the cowboy anymore, but Archie the delinquent with his afflicted mother and dead father, with all his crimes against society. Honest, it makes me feel like crap.

Good thing that's a feeling that doesn't last long. I can hang up the phone, go to bed, sleep like a dead man, give Richard a hundred-watt smile when he rousts me out of bed, ready to get out on the open range and make those cows pay.

I've just come into town from shoveling about three tons of cowshit out at the loading corrals and now I'm here in a bar called Whirly Burly's (the guy at the door didn't card me; because of my six-four frame and five-o'clock shadow I haven't been carded since I was fourteen). I've decided to go through with it, I won't wait any longer: I'm going to locate Calfred Pulsipher and let him have it. I figured the natural place to look for him would be a bar; the man was a full-time drunk and I doubt he's changed his ways. But, I have to admit, this doesn't seem the kind of place you'd find somebody like Calfred Pulsipher, full as it is with a bunch of yahoos dressed up like they're waiting to audition for *Oklahoma!*

As I search the crowd, looking for something like the face I saw in the paper, I have this heavy, sick feeling in my gut. What if I do see him? What am I going to do? I've thought a lot about this, especially in the past few days, I've gone over and over it in my mind. My plan is simple and just: I'll do it to him the way he did it to my father: I'll pick a fight. I will *make* him fight me. The only difference is I won't need to use a forty-pound jack to finish him off.

But what about afterwards? Don't think I haven't considered that. Calfred Pulsipher killed my father and wasn't even given a trial. An autopsy was done and they said they could not infallibly trace the bleeding to any of the blows he received. Small town, bogus bullshit. My mother kept all the newspaper clippings and they tell the whole story; the way they saw it, two good old boys got drunk, had a bit of a scuffle, and one of them had the misfortune of getting killed.

Sending somebody to jail wouldn't make anything better, would it? Why make a bad situation worse?

Just thinking about it makes my blood go lava-hot and I want to grab the chair I'm in and start smashing things and people. Even if I get thrown in the clink, *even* if they send me there forever, I've got to go through with it. I owe it to my father. I owe it to my mother and to myself. It's the one thing I want to get right in this fucked-up life of mine.

I sip my Dr. Pepper and watch people pushing through the big swinging wooden doors and each time I get this needle-jab of dread in my chest, thinking it might be him, but it's only these assholes in their creased blue jeans. Honest, I'd like to line them up and whale the shit out of them, one by one, just for practice. And this music they all listen to. I may like the cowboy life but nobody says I have to listen to their music.

Everyone starts clearing chairs and lining up to do these ridiculous syncopated honky-tonk dance steps. Even though I smell like the end of civilization and I'm not wearing Tony Lamas and a shiny belt buckle the size of a dessert plate, a few of these swivel-hipped cowgirls with moisture in their cleavages come up and ask me to dance. I put on my best smile and politely decline; I have a lot on my mind.

I sit there and watch the clumps of young men crowded together, slamming beers and cat-calling the women, and for the first time since I've been in Arizona I feel lonely and a little homesick, sitting here by myself in a bar roaring with people having a good time.

Before going home I hit the remaining bars in Salado, all four of them, but there is not a sign of Calfred Pulsipher. When I drag my ass back to the trailer it's nearly one a.m. and I can see through the window that Richard, clad in camouflage-style long johns, has fallen asleep in his recliner with the Volume A encyclopedia nestled in his groin. I know he is waiting up for me; he wants to be the one to catch me when I slip up.

I'm tired but I don't feel like dealing with Richard, so I take a walk up the hill toward the ranch house. Though I hadn't meant to, I end up standing on the front lawn of the house, looking up at the dark windows, thinking: I used to live in this house. It is white, two-storied and has a wide covered porch with a built-in swinging love seat. In the nine months I've been here I've never stepped foot in this house, never really had any desire to, until now.

I walk around the place a couple of times, tripping over a Big Wheel, nearly falling into one of those plastic baby-pools, and finally I decide—what can it hurt?—to take a look inside. The only first-floor window I can find that doesn't have the shades drawn is back behind a thick mass of bushes. I use a breast-stroke swimming motion to claw my way in and find myself looking into what is probably the family room: pictures on the wall, a cowhide couch, a grandfather clock, a collection of old Coca-Cola bottles on the mantel. Everything is dark and shadowed, but I try to imagine what the room would look like in the light of day, what my mother—a young, pretty version—might have looked like sitting on the couch, or my father over in the corner, winding the clock.

I strain, I try, but nothing; I can't seem to jog a single memory. Then, just as I'm pulling myself out of the bushes, I hear something behind me and there's Ted in nothing but boxer shorts and unlaced running shoes holding a .22 pistol. His legs and chest are the color of mayonnaise.

"Hey," he says, squinting. He's not wearing his glasses and I can tell he doesn't know who I am—I think about making a break for it. Finally, I whisper, "Ted, it's Archie."

Ted fiddles with one of his hearing aids and says, "Archie?"

"Couldn't sleep," I say. "I'm out for a walk."

"Is there something wrong?" Ted says. "Something you need to talk about?"

I think of the questions I would love to ask Ted: *What was my father like when you knew him? Do we really have the same looks, the same way of talking? When you moved into the house did it smell like English Leather?* But I keep my mouth shut.

Ted looks at me for a minute, as if he's trying to make some kind of decision, and then he says, "That Miss Condley woman called tonight. She tried calling over to your place but you weren't there all night. She was pretty upset."

"Shit," I say. I'd completely forgotten it was Tuesday, the day Ms. Condley calls every week.

"Five o'clock's a bitch, Archie," Ted says, turning around to go inside. "I'd get to bed if I was you."

On my way to the trailer a wave of exhaustion hits me and I can barely put one foot in front of the other. Careful not to wake Richard, I check in on Doug who is pacing the floor of the laundry room like an expectant father, back and forth, back and forth, no doubt full of worries of his own—an insomniac if there ever was one. I pick him up and take him to bed with me. I lie under the covers and hold him tight against my chest—this kind of pressure calms him for some reason—and pretty soon he's making this gurgling noise in the back of his throat, almost like the purring of a cat. When he's good and relaxed I put him up on the bedpost where he hunkers right down and nods off. Crazy as it sounds, it comforts me to have him there, above me in the dark while I sleep.

Instead of lounging on the couch watching *Cheers* after work, I'm driving hell-bent-for-leather in a lavender Oldsmobile packed with illegal aliens. My blood is hopped up with adrenaline and I'm doing well over seventy with an old Mexican woman asleep in my lap.

This all started last night after surveying the bars and my little run-in with Ted. I barely got to sleep and the next thing I knew there was Jesus, right in my bedroom, tugging on my big toe. "Arshie," he whispered. "Wake it up."

I could tell right away something was the matter; instead of that what-the-hell grin he always wears, his face was pinched and worried. And what's more, he'd once vowed never to step foot in a residence which housed a "big dirty-shit buzzard," as he put it. But here he was.

He jabbered in a mixture of English and Spanish and finally I got the gist of the problem; his family was stuck at the border. Jesus' wife and kids go down to visit family once or twice a year and they've always had someone, a contact, who would arrange for them to get across the border, bribe the right people, and drive them up to Salado. Now apparently, that contact had disappeared and the family was waiting at the border down near Nogales; Jesus had made arrangements for them to get across but there was nobody to pick them up. Jesus himself couldn't risk going; not only did he not have a driver's license (if he was stopped on the highway he'd end up on the other side of the border, too), he was supposed to go with Ted to the livestock auction in Albuquerque.

He pulled a fist-sized wad of money out of his pocket. "I pay big cash."

I pushed the wad away and told him he was insulting me with his money. What was a favor between friends? Jesus eyed me like he thought I was crazy, then began outlining what he wanted me to do.

My work today involved digging out several cattle guards and I worked like a man on fire to get done early. I finished by four o'clock, drove the Ford home, and there was the '72 Oldsmobile sitting out in front of the trailer just as Jesus said it would be. He had borrowed the car from his Aunt Lourdes, and I figured it would be an inconspicuous looking vehicle, but this one looked like a pimp/drug pusher special. The damn thing was about as long as your average school bus and *purple*.

It drove like a champ, though. It's a four-hour drive down to Nogales but I made it in just under three, the huge rosary on the rearview mirror clacking against the windshield the whole way. By the time I got there it was just getting dark and starting to drizzle. I had no trouble finding the spot Jesus described to me; about eight miles west of Nogales a small utility road runs parallel to the twelve-foot border fence, which is intersected by some railroad tracks. Above the tracks two red warning lights cast their glow over everything, making you feel like you're in hell.

I had assumed that the family would be there, already across, but the place was as quiet and empty as the rest of the desert. I could hear coyotes shouting at each other off in the distance.

I sat there a good hour, seeing nothing, hearing nothing but the coyotes, getting more worried by the minute. With the racket the coyotes were making, and the perfect stillness of everything else, along with the red glow of the lights, I got paranoid. I was scared, I'll admit it. I wanted to fire up that long purple machine and get the hell away. On the way down I'd worried about getting back in time for Ms. Condley to call; since she missed me last night I knew she would be calling tonight, and being out of the house again would look suspicious. But now I was simply spooked about getting caught; it's not something I've checked on, but transporting illegal aliens is most likely a felony and would land me in some serious shit.

I got out of the car, pacing around in the mud, stopping to listen once in awhile, until I heard what sounded like a car motor out in the dark. I strained my ears and after awhile I heard voices that sounded like they were coming from the other side of the fence. About a hundred yards off, in a shallow ravine, I saw movement. I crept closer and could just make out somebody working on the fence with what looked like a pair of wire-cutters.

I counted ten people coming under, a few of them children. When I agreed to pick up Jesus' family, I thought he meant his wife and kids, not the whole bunch. They all started off in the opposite direction from me, lugging shopping sacks full of belongings. It was obvious they could not see me so I flashed my headlights to let them know where I was. Immediately someone swore in Spanish and everyone began running towards the car, shouting and bumping into each other. About halfway to the car, one of the kids, apparently spooked and bewildered by this whole affair, peeled off to the left and began running helter-skelter through the brush. I went after him, using a little cowboy geometry; when going after a steer you don't pursue him directly, you estimate where his path will take him and you head out for that point. The kid, however, didn't cooperate, zigzagging like a rabbit under fire, with me high-stepping it through the mud behind him, clown-like.

By the time I was able to corral the kid and carry him back to the car, everyone had most of their belongings stuffed into the trunk, themselves jammed in the car, and some old lady was at the wheel, cranking the key and gunning the accelerator. I convinced her to scoot over and let me take the controls, and just as we started out, a pair of headlights with a search beam on top came over a hill about half a mile away. Who knows, it could have been some redneck out spotlighting deer, but at that moment I was sure the border patrol, the FBI and CIA were all bearing down on us. Everyone shouted at once and the grandma put up a high-pitched wail, the kind you hear at third-world funerals. The car fishtailed in the mud and lumbered over clumps of cactus and mesquite; I kept the lights off so I had no idea where I was going. I'm a veteran of chases like these, but this time I was scared out of my mind, pretty much like everybody else in the car. Somebody in back prayed to the Virgin Mary, the kids screamed, Grandma wailed, and for once in my life I kept perfectly quiet.

It didn't take long for my eyes to adjust to the darkness and pretty soon I found myself on a washboard dirt road heading god-knows-where. A couple of times we saw headlights, way off in the distance, which made the Grandma start up her wail, inducing the kids in back to commence their crying again.

But now, after about a half hour of searching, we've got ourselves back on the highway and everybody seems to have calmed. Grandma is so relaxed she's snoring like a lumberjack. By the time we make it to Salado, it's near midnight and pretty much everybody in the car except me is asleep. When I pull into Jesus' front yard, I can see him sitting under the old basketball hoop, his hands clamped together between his legs. I pull to a stop, shut off the engine and suddenly it's chaos again, people shouting and trying to untangle themselves, babies crying, Grandma giving orders.

As I help pull belongings out of the trunk I watch Jesus gather his two daughters and little son, hugging them, not willing to let go even though they are already squirming to get away. I know this is a common scene, a father being reunited with his kids, but for some reason, standing there in the dark of the other side of the car, I have to turn away. I look in the other direction, out at the lights of town, until Jesus comes up behind me and gives me a good whack on the back, saying, "Tank you, Arshie, very good," and holding a hand over his heart.

He invites me inside, but his tiny house is already over-
flowing with people, so I ask him if I can take the Oldsmobile
out for a drive. I've only had a couple hours of sleep in the last
two days but I don't feel like going back to the trailer. Jesus
says no problem, take the car to Las Vegas if you want.

I drive into Salado and stop at Burly's; I feel like talking to
someone, blowing off a little steam, but the place is nearly
empty tonight. Only a few old-timers sit at the bar, bending
down to their shot glasses like birds drinking from a puddle.
I take a table near the back and I sit there alone for a minute.
I keep seeing that scene with Jesus and his kids and I feel so
clenched and jumpy it's like I'm going to explode. So when
the bartender calls over the bar, asking what do I want, without much hesitation I call back, "Shot of Jim Beam."

When the drink comes, I look at it for a minute before I lift
it to my mouth. It's been less than a year since I had a drink,
but the stuff scorches my throat like it's my first time ever. I
sip the whiskey, swishing it around, and by the time I'm
halfway finished with my second shot I've decided—it's
almost like a revelation—that tonight is the night I'm going
to take care of Calfred Pulsipher. I could wait around forever
for him to come out of hiding, checking the bars, looking
under every hat at the gas station and grocery store, or I could
have some real-man balls and go directly to him.

Suddenly I can't stay a minute longer in that place, not even
for a few more drinks, so I drop some money on the table, get
into the car, and stop in at the Circle K for a six-pack. Then
I'm on my way back to Jesus' house.

When I get there, the house is entirely dark. I figured
everybody would still be up, celebrating or something, but the
place is quiet as a tomb. Without meaning to I pound so hard
on the door the whole house shakes.

I see a teenage girl—one of my passengers earlier tonight—

peek through the window and then Jesus comes out, pants unzipped, shirt on inside-out. I can smell the damp scent of sex on him and there's no doubt I've just broken up the long-awaited reunion with his wife. He's in there putting that big pecker of his to good use and along comes Archie in the middle of the night to break things up.

I feel stupid and guilty, but I'm not going to let that stop me. "Jesus," I say, "I'm real sorry but I need you to tell me where Calfred Pulsipher lives."

"Ah?" Jesus says, peering out at me.

"I need to know where Calfred Pulsipher lives. Please."

"Now? You going there now?"

"Right now."

Jesus sighs, shouts back something inside to his wife, closes the door and steps outside next to me.

"Why you going there?" he says.

"All you have to do is tell me where."

"Come on," Jesus says, walking barefoot across the gravel and bullheads. He gets in his work truck and says, "I bring you."

I try to tell him that he only needs to give me directions, but he shakes his head, revs the engine, and says, "Come in."

I feel like cockroach shit for taking advantage of him like this, doing him a favor and then asking one in return right off the bat, ruining his night and everything. I try to tell him this on the way but he waves his hand at me without looking my way. I break one of the beers off the six-pack and hand it to him and he tosses it right out the window.

We're on the highway for a couple of miles before Jesus turns off on a tiny dirt road I've never noticed before. It's barely a cow track, full of mudholes and melon-sized boulders. Jesus keeps the truck on a straight course, heedless of the obstacles, and the truck jounces and rocks like a boat in high

seas. I tear off one of the beers for myself; the whiskey I drank
at Burly's hardly did a thing for me, and I know I'll need to be
good and whacked-out to get through this whole thing, but
the beer tastes sour and watery, and with all the bouncing
around this truck is doing, I'm this close to throwing up all
over the floor. So I chuck the remainder of the six-pack out
the window, as far as it will go, and watch the cans jump and
spray among the bushes. After what seems like miles of bump
and rattle, Jesus turns again on another dirt road and suddenly stops.

"What's wrong?" I say.

"Here," he says.

I look around, seeing nothing but brush and slab-sided
buttes, and then I notice the shell of an old Buick sitting back
off the road about thirty yards, and behind that, in the night-
shadows of an old cottonwood, is a house no bigger than a rich
man's bathroom. I look back at Jesus, who's staring out the
windshield, and get out of the truck.

Walking toward that house it's like I'm a ghost, floating,
nothing but air. I can't feel my feet touch the ground. I try not
to think about what I'm doing, what I'm going to do. Once
I'm within ten feet or so I can see that the house is a ram-
shackle adobe affair, mud showing through holes in the stucco. Somebody has done their best to make the place look nice,
the tiny, half-dead lawn cluttered with ceramic elves, ducks
whose wings spin when the wind blows, birdbaths and plastic
sunflowers.

I step up on the porch and give the screen door three good
raps. A long, sick minute passes before I hear someone shuffling along the floor. The porch light clicks on, the door opens
toward me and somebody leans half into the light.

It takes me a moment to recognize Calfred Pulsipher.
Instead of the young man in the newspaper picture, or the

even younger man I've seen in my father's old yearbooks, this Calfred Pulsipher looks like he belongs in an old folk's home. His hair is thin and colorless, his back bowed, his skin papery and stained with coffee-colored blotches. An oxygen tube, strapped around his head, feeds into both his nostrils. He's pulling a wheeled tank behind him with one hand and in the other he's holding a rusty sawed-off shotgun, pointed at my stomach.

The light blinds him for a moment and he squints at me, bracing the screen door with his elbow. We stand there like that, two feet apart, staring at each other, until his eyes suddenly go wide, his mouth opens slowly, forming a circle, and he says, "Oh."

The gun slides out of his hand, bouncing off the threshold and clattering against the oxygen tank.

I can't do anything but look from his right eye, which is locked on me, burning and wet, to his left, which is swiveling around in his head like a thing that's got a mind of its own. His brows are pushed up and together and his mouth is opening and closing without any sound.

He takes one stumbling step toward me, arms out. One of his knees buckles under him and he grabs my shirt, pulling himself back up, leaning into me, reaching up and putting his arms around my shoulders. I can feel his whiskers on my neck and I don't know if the strong, bitter smell of alcohol is coming from him or me. He holds his head against my collarbone, moving it back and forth, saying, "Oh, oh."

It would be so easy, all I would have to do is return his embrace, crush him in my arms until his bones cracked and his worthless lungs gave out. But I can't do it. I can't. My whole body feels numb and my hands are at my sides, as heavy and useless as hub caps.

He hangs on me like that, until Jesus steps out of the shadows and pulls me away. Jesus leads me back towards the truck and I make it only ten steps or so until I fall forward, my whole body gone limp with shame and relief. I catch myself with my hands and begin coughing into the dirt, it's like there are chunks of black matter dislodging themselves from deep inside, stuff that has been there forever is coming up, and I can't stop, my stomach heaving, and I begin to weep. I can't remember ever crying in my entire life, but I'm making up for it now, my sinuses burning with tears, my throat constricting on me, and I go like that, hacking and retching, unable to breathe, until I vomit violently into a clump of sagebrush.

Jesus stands over me, his hand on my back, and he says quietly, "Come on, Arshie. Get it up."

He wipes off my mouth with his shirt, helps me to my feet, and with his arm locked in mine, we start again for the truck. I look back and the last thing I see is Calfred Pulsipher still standing in the light, like a man caught in the bright beam of a spaceship.

The ride home is nothing more than a dense fog moving past, and when we get back to the trailer Doug is in the front room, waddling around in the dark like some deformed duck, picking crumbs off the carpet. Jesus kicks him out of the way, and Doug goes flapping toward the kitchen, a few black feathers coming loose. Jesus sits me down on the couch and asks me if I want him to stay with me. I tell him to get his ass on home where his wife is waiting for him to finish the job he'd started and he is out the door in a heartbeat.

Richard appears in his bedroom doorway, wearing his camo-pajamas, his hair smashed against one side of his head. "Hey, Ms. Condley called again," he says. "Sounds like you're in a little trouble."

"Ms. Condley can go to hell," I say, not caring whether

Richard notices my puffy eyes or the thickness in my voice. "And so can you, for that matter."

Once Richard retreats to his room, I go and get Doug, who is sulking under the kitchen table, and take him outside. The sky has cleared and the stars are shining down and even though I've slept only a few minutes in the past few days, even though I'm exhausted and weak, there is still something inside me that needs to be released; I want to open up my lungs and shout like a maniac, wake everyone for miles. Instead, I take Doug in the crook of my arm and walk up the hill past the ranch house, which is glowing a faint, moonlit blue, all the way down to the mud pond where a few steers are standing around, rubbing their heads together. It's become such a bright night there's no difficulty at all in finding the anchor post, the one with my father's initial. I squat down next to that post and bite into it, hard, right near the Q. I bite so hard the muscles in my jaw begin to burn and I come away with a taste in my mouth of wood and salt and dust. I stand up, holding Doug close, looking down at the indentations my teeth made and a feeling of pride and certainty rises up in me. There is no doubt in my mind: this is my place, it's where I belong, and I'm here to stay.